Simon Crisp on the British way of sex?
Surely it's got to be a joke . . .

Monday, 22 January

Never having been to a sex film, am not quite sure where to begin. Should one break oneself in with something fairly innocuous like *Flesh Gordon* or *Emmanuelle Meets the Wife Swappers* and gradually work one's way up towards the meatier stuff? Or should one go straight for the hard core and get the worst over as soon as possible?

Sue absolutely no help whatever. Posed my dilemma to her over a cup of coffee soon after getting in this morning.

She said, 'I have never felt the slightest desire to see any films of that sort, hard, soft, or otherwise, and neither, I'm glad to say, have any of my friends, so I'm afraid I can't help you.'

Reminded her in no uncertain terms that this was neither the time nor the place for a display of her Home County scruples and that, as my full-time assistant, I expected her co-operation at all times.

I said, 'You don't suppose I'm in this for fun, do you?'

THE CRISP REPORT

Christopher Matthew

ARROW BOOKS

To Bridge and Al, with love

Arrow Books Limited
17–21 Conway Street, London W1P 6JD

An imprint of the Hutchinson Publishing Group

London Melbourne Sydney Auckland
Johannesburg and agencies
throughout the world

First published 1981
Arrow edition 1982

© Christopher Matthew 1981

Made and printed in Great Britain
by The Anchor Press Ltd
Tiptree, Essex

ISBN 0 09 929180 0

Memo

From: The Chairman
To: All Departments   2 January

This is to confirm that, pursuant upon the unexpected departure of Mr Harold Hill, the following appointments have been made:

Keith Hardacre, from Marketing Director to Deputy Managing Director, effective immediately.

Simon Crisp, from Department Market Manager to Special Projects Manager, this to take effect on his return from the USA.

My dear Angela,

Just a brief note to apologize once again for the unfortunate scene at the Dongs' Howdee Neighbours' party on New Year's Day, and to say how very sorry I am that things between us did not turn out quite as well as we had both hoped and expected. Please apologize to Harry and Deedee on my behalf. I shall be writing in due course, but in the meantime, if Harry would like to forward me the bill for the new water jug, I'll settle up with him forthwith.

As you know, I enjoy Sportsnight with Coleman as much as the next man. However, in my book, there is more to a relationship than that.

The point is, Angela, one's got to have something to do between the hanky-panky, and I'm sorry to say that I think that your suggestion that one should sit about planning the next session does not altogether fit the bill as far as I am concerned.

As you know, my idea of travel is getting out and about among the highways and byways, observing the natives in their natural habitats and generally acquainting myself with their customs and way of life. Plonk me down at a busy pavement café with a notebook and pencil and a glass of dry white wine and I'm as happy as a sandman. In that way I suppose I'm a bit of a Freya Stark or Jan Morris.

Pope was right. The proper study of mankind *is* man. But not the way you mean.

Home is where the heart is and much as I would have liked to tell you to the contrary, I did not leave mine in San Francisco. London very much belongs to me, I realize that now. Which brings me on to my latest bit of news, and pretty sensational it is too.

As you know, I was convinced that, once the chairman, Harold Hill, had eloped to France with Pippa Robinson, it was only a matter of time before the knives were not only out but deeply embedded in my back. I had pinned my colours to Harold's mast pretty firmly and heads were bound to roll. It was like the abdication crisis all over again with myself in the Fruity Metcalfe role.

However, arrived in my office to find a memo from Keith Hardacre announcing that not only had he been promoted to Deputy Managing Director but that I, too, had been promoted – to the post of Special Projects Manager. This means not just a 15% rise in salary, but also a decent office at the front of the building overlooking the square, possibly a secretary of my own, and a key to the Seven Above Club – the bar on the top floor of No. 7 that only the top executives in the firm are permitted to use. Quite a feather in my cap, I think you'll agree.

My first project, if you can believe the irony of it, is to compile a special report on sex in Britain today. I am to get cracking on it straight away and the whole thing is to be delivered by the end of February. As you can imagine, I immediately rang Hardacre for an explanation.

He said, 'It is twenty-one years since the *Lady Chatterley's Lover* trial heralded the permissive society. We at Barfords think it is high time someone in this country came up with a progress report on the current state of British mores. We believe that Barfords are exactly the right sort of people to carry out a study of this sort.'

I reminded him that the Williams Committee had recently spent several years producing an excellent report along very much the same lines.

Hardacre said, 'Good point, but the fact is that we want the Crisp Report to go a good deal further than Williams and cover the entire field of sexual behaviour. Obscenity is only the tip of the iceberg, to our way of thinking.'

I could hardly believe my ears. The Crisp Report! Naturally I have every intention of accepting – once I've got my committee together, that is.

I am hardly what you might call a Masters or a Johnson. I must pass through Soho half a dozen times a week and yet never once have I felt the slightest urge to enter a porno cinema or witness a live sex show or call upon the services of a 'young model'.

Tant pis for me, some may say, and they are probably right. It is, after all, the duty of every intelligent responsible citizen with the slightest claim to a social conscience to acquaint himself with every aspect of modern life, including the soft underbelly of the consumer society. Having been afforded this unique opportunity I cannot wait to get started.

My only real concern is that my friends – and, more importantly, Mother – should not get hold of the wrong end of the stick and jump to the conclusion that I have taken this thing on in order to satisfy some personal need or gratification.

Frankly I have better things to do with my time than waste it on the massage parlours and peep shows of London's so-called Golden Mile. However, I have always held that, if a job's worth doing, it's worth doing well, and I believe that to rub shoulders with the twilight world of bottoms and breasts can only serve to increase one's understanding of this funny old world in which we live.

Must close now and get ahead with my committee short-list. Am wondering if John Mortimer would consider helping out in an ex officio capacity. He is very much in the public eye these days and I have always been a great fan of his.

My best to the Dongs, and don't forget about the jug, will you?

Affectionately,
Simon

PS I didn't happen to leave a pair of underpants lying around, did I? I seem to be short and can't think where they could be otherwise. If you do come across them, perhaps you would be kind enough to pop them in a strong manilla envelope? I will, of course, reimburse the postage costs.

Confidential Memo

From: Simon Crisp, Special Projects Manager
To: Keith Hardacre, Deputy Managing Director
                                        10 January
Re: *Crisp Report Committee*

I have given this matter a lot of thought and my proposals are as follows: I should, of course, wish you and Neville to be as closely involved in the project as possible. I have been most impressed, as I know you have, by Roger Fremantle's work on the in-house magazine. We need a good editorial mind on this. I do not know what the form is re involving Harley Preston. However, my feeling is that we do not make full enough use of our marketing consultants, and Colin Armitage is one of the few people I know who is genuinely *au fait* with the sexual world. Shall I progress this or will you? I feel a female mind might have something useful to contribute, and who better than the chairman's secretary, Erica? She and her husband live near Bromley. Enough said?

Am considering the possibility of approaching John Mortimer in an advisory capacity. Ditto Clement Freud. To have a sympathetic foot in the Palace of Westminster might be very useful.

May I have your reactions to this at the earliest possible opportunity?

S.c.

Memo

To: Simon Crisp
From: Keith Hardacre   15 January

Someone's lines seem to have been crossed somewhere. All this talk of a committee is news to me. My idea was simply that you should pop into a few sex films, skim through some magazines, and collate some rough statistics on wife swapping, adultery, etc. It may have escaped your notice, but we are in the middle of a recession and we shall have to keep a close watch on every penny if we are to come through it in one piece. To give you some idea of the gravity of the situation, we are scrapping the Seven Above Club. In the circumstances, therefore, while we are 100% behind you over this one, the idea of a redistribution of manpower along the lines you suggest would be quite out of the question.

If you feel you are not up to it, please say so immediately and we will start looking round for someone else. I should value your reply within the week.

Memo

From: Simon
To: Keith   16 January

May I call upon the services of a full-time secretary?

S.c.

Memo

From: Mr Hardacre
To: Mr Crisp   17 January

I have arranged for Sue Frizzell to be seconded to your
department on a temporary basis.

KH

Memo

From: Simon Crisp, Special Projects Manager
To: Keith Hardacre, Deputy Managing Director
cc: Neville Pratt, Personnel, Accounts, File

18 January

Re: *The Crisp Report*

This is to confirm that, as from today, 18 January, I shall
be working full-time on the above-mentioned study into
the contemporary state of British mores, with direct
responsibility to you.

S.c.

Private and Confidential Memo

From: Simon
To: Keith   18 January

Just a small point, between ourselves.

When you said in your memo that you wanted me to
'pop into a few sex films, skim through some magazines,
and collate some rough statistics on wife swapping, adultery, etc.', what exactly did you have in mind and how far
precisely do you want me to go?

Re massage parlours, for instance. Do you think it absolutely crucial to the authenticity of the report that I actually have a 'massage' and all that that entails? Does one really need to sit through hours of hard-core films, or would an interview with a leading pornographer fit the bill just as well? Naturally, not having a wife, it would be impossible for me to swap one with someone else's, but my not being married certainly does not preclude me technically from committing adultery. But how far is one expected to go in the interests of truth? I feel one should draw the line somewhere, but where exactly?

I look forward to your comments at the earliest opportunity.

S.c.

Memo

To: Simon Crisp
From: Keith Hardacre   19 January

Re your memo, I leave it entirely to your discretion.

Please note that I shall be away on a skiing holiday from noon today until Monday, 29 January. I look forward to your progress report then.

R. Hippo
pp. Keith Hardacre
Dictated by Mr Hardacre and signed in his absence.

Progress Report to Myself

Saturday

I know now how Winston Churchill must have felt in 1940 when he was summoned to the Palace and asked by the King if he would be prepared to form a government. He wrote at the time that he felt as if he were walking with destiny and as if his whole life had been but a prelude to that moment – and so do I. A short stint in the wilderness never did anyone any harm.

Where though to begin? Once again I find myself regretting Beddoes' disappearance to Brussels. For all his endless succession of inconsiderate and humourless inamoratae, and his fondness for jokes based upon the lavatory, my ex-flatmate was extremely knowledgeable concerning the grubbier areas of life about which most of us are, thank goodness, ignorant.

Still, I have a feeling he was planning to come to London some time in the next few weeks. I might very well drop him a line and suggest picking his brains over a rather good lunch (or, knowing his strange tastes in food, picking a rather good lunch over his brains). Ditto Tim Pedalow and possibly the awful Colin Armitage. I cannot really believe that Hugh Bryant-Fenn will have any first-hand experiences to offer, since his most personal relationship to date appears to have been with his late pet budgerigar, Percy. However, in this life there are those who do and those who know people who do, and Hugh certainly knows a few people one way and another. I've no idea who, but it can't do any harm to drop him a line.

In the meantime, I shall get on with some basic field research. Am still slightly in the dark as to the form my report should take. I daresay the nature of the material itself will determine this. Have decided to jot down all my researches in a notebook willy-nilly. Although have told Hardacre am beginning with sex shops, think I shall seize the sexual bull by the horns and plunge straight into the world of sex films.

Monday, 22 January

Never having been to a sex film, am not quite sure where to begin. Should one break oneself in with something fairly innocuous like *Flesh Gordon* or *Emmanuelle Meets the Wife Swappers* and gradually work one's way up towards the meatier stuff? Or should one go straight for the hard-core and get the worst over as soon as possible?

Sue absolutely no help whatever. Posed my dilemma to her over a cup of coffee soon after getting in this morning.

She said, 'I have never felt the slightest desire to see any films of that sort, hard, soft or otherwise, and neither, I'm glad to say, have any of my friends, so I'm afraid I can't help you.'

Reminded her in no uncertain terms that this was neither the time nor the place for a display of her Home County scruples and that, as my full-time assistant, I expected her co-operation at all times.

I said, 'You don't suppose I'm in this for fun, do you?'

'I don't see why not,' she said. 'Anyone else I know would be.'

I can see that someone's going to have to read the riot act to someone before very long.

Lunched modestly off a toasted sardine sandwich, then set off to Soho for a preliminary recce.

Had not realized before how many porno cinemas there are in this part of London. Interested to see that the word 'Swedish' features a good deal in neon. Quite why this should be, I do not know. If the de Grande-Hautevilles' au pair is anything to go by, the average Swedish girl is sulky, unalluring, and about as sexy as a cup of cold Horlicks.

Outside La Continentale in Wardour Street was a sign saying: 'This cinema is showing uncensored films of a sexual and explicit nature. Any person who may be offended or shocked by this type of material should not enter this cinema.'

How the initiate is to know if he is going to be offended or shocked without having a look first, I cannot imagine. Was jotting down exact wording in a notebook when a dark-skinned fellow with a heavy moustache, a gold chain nestling among a jungle of chest hair, and accent of vaguely eastern Mediterranean extraction, strolled out of entrance and came up to me and asked if there was anything I wanted. I replied that I was merely taking down a few particulars.

'Look,' he said, 'no children in this cinema.'

'I should hope not,' I said.

'No animals,' he said.

I said with a laugh, 'You can't take your dog anywhere these days.'

He frowned and said, 'You from West End Central?'

'No,' I said. 'From Barfords actually. You may have heard of us.' I explained about the report.

He said, 'You sure you're not from the police? Mrs Whitesides? GLC?'

I shook my head.

He said, 'I don't know who you are or what you want, but I run a respectable cinema here. All completely above the line, you know?'

I said, 'This is most interesting. When you say respectable, what do you mean exactly?'

He seized me by the arm. 'Look,' he said. 'If you want to see the show, see the show, be my guest. But please, don't stand here writing in your little book. It's bad for business.'

I explained that unfortunately I had an important meeting to attend, but that I certainly hoped to sample his wares at a later date along with the rest of the paying public.

He said, 'Please yourself,' and disappeared inside.

Doubt if I shall in fact take him up on his offer. Am convinced that in any form of research anonymity is very much a *sine qua non*. One cannot imagine Egon Ronay turning up out of the blue at Le Gavroche and demanding a free meal, and while I am not for a moment suggesting that the manager of La Continentale would have attempted to get into my good books by laying on a few 'special' items, I do not believe one can get a properly balanced view without experiencing it from the public's point of view. Also, one has to be careful dealing with the underworld. Lay yourself open to bribery and corruption and suddenly you'll find you're being asked to repay the favour at a most inconvenient moment. We at Barfords cannot afford to be caught up in a squalid blackmail situation.

Decided I was not yet up to material of this strength and that I really would do better to kick off with something a bit milder.

Sat down in snack bar with cup of tea, Kit-Kat and the *New Standard* and began browsing through entertainments pages. Unfortunately, titles gave very little hint as to the content of the films on offer. One film, *Phantasm*, carried with it the promise (or possibly threat) 'Sex will never be the same again.' Is one to understand from this that those who see the film will find their personal lives altered in some dramatic fashion? Or does the phrase have a wider significance? Have all our lives been in some mysterious way transformed by one film? Have made a mental note to have a look in the next time I am passing.

Further down the page, my eye was caught by the news that the Cinecenta at Piccadilly Circus was showing the first ever Triple-X programme, comprising *The True Blue Confessions of Mary Millington*, plus *Boys and Girls Together*, and *Scandinavian Erotica* – an 'X-certificate shocker – includes scenes from hard-core movies previously banned for general viewing'.

This sounded very much the sort of thing I ought to be cutting my sexual teeth on.

Was paying my £2.90 at Cinecenta box office when suddenly remembered this was the same cinema I had once visited many years ago, which had a little balcony to one side of the auditorium where they served light teas during the performance. The combination of *Nudes in the Snow* and a toasted tea cake is an experience I shall always treasure.

Sadly, the old place has undergone the indignity suffered by all cinemas these days of being sliced up into a series of long, thin rooms, so that one has the sense of watching a film in a hotel corridor.

Not that either *Blue Confessions* or *Scandinavian Erotica* would have looked or sounded any the better by being shown in the Odeon, Leicester Square.

The highlight of the proceedings came when Mary Millington, once a popular sex star, declared, 'It's not the sleep of the just that counts; it's the sleep of the just after.'

No one laughed though. They were probably all asleep. I know I nearly was.

Was interested to note that, in the interval, despite the fact that I am a lifelong choc-ice man, found myself going instinctively for a cone – something I have not done since childhood. Man in next seat ate two! It just goes to show the sort of effect a short exposure to pornography can have on even the strongest-minded amongst us without our realizing it. Goodness knows how I shall react when I start getting down to the real hard-core stuff, though have a feeling they may not sell ice creams in this kind of cinema.

Decided to put the interval to good use by making a spot survey of the sort of people who make up the audiences in the Jaceys, the Cinecentas and the Moulins of Britain.

Of the thirty or so present, half appeared to be Chinese waiters – on their afternoon off, I daresay. Of the remainder 40% were in the 45–65 age bracket, and, in socio-economic terms, C1/C2/D, at a rough guess. The rest were quite young couples. The pair in front of me were very lovey-dovey and I made a mental note to keep my eye on them to see if the nature of the entertainment had any interesting effects on them.

Was halfway through a rough head-count of rainwear when the lights dimmed and *Boys and Girls Together* started.

The story was set in London. It began, like *Scandinavian Erotica*, with an aeroplane landing. Am wondering if these sex film producers have some sort of tie-in with the airlines. If we're not careful, they'll soon be giving us in-flight blue movies.

The hero, a young American, was soon through customs and on his way to Hampstead, where he appeared to have fixed himself up in advance with accommodation in a large Victorian house.

The house had six rooms. Number 1 was occupied by a black man doing press-ups; 2, by a nude blonde having a shower; 3, by a long-haired Japanese youth thumbing through a pansy magazine; 4, by a black girl eating a banana; and 5, by a dopey-looking white girl sitting on the loo.

No sooner had the American set foot in his room than he was thumbing through a girlie magazine.

After a while, we saw the loo lady ironing a pair of

panties. The Japanese, who had a kitten, was washing his. (Panties, that is, not kitten.) The blonde, whose name was Ilsa, was listening to the wireless.

The black man stared gloomily for a long time at a photograph of a rather frumpy black girl (his girlfriend back home in Trinidad presumably, but possibly his mother) before suddenly snatching it off the wall and tearing it into shreds.

The black girl in No. 4, meanwhile, was sticking up a poster of the pop singer Roger Daltrey, and in No. 3 the Japanese was enjoying an extremely satisfying dream about a young fellow-countryman playing tennis.

No one, it seemed, had pressing engagements, or regular employment. Perhaps it was the weekend.

There then followed a sensational chain of events.

First, the white girl slipped on a bar of soap in the bathroom and gave herself a cheap and unexpected thrill with the loo brush. Next, the black man found the kitten wandering around the corridor and took it back to its Japanese owner who, by way of saying thank you, invited the somewhat bemused fellow on to the bed to join him in some hanky-panky.

Meanwhile in No. 4, the coloured girl had fallen in love with a huge carrot while preparing herself a salad lunch.

The American, miraculously transported to Soho, was enjoying a good deal less luck. But then anyone who hands over twenty pounds to a tart in the street is asking for trouble and even I, who know nothing of these things, could have told him she was going to make a run for it.

Back in Hampstead, Ilsa and the other white girl were contriving to brush against each other a good deal in the bathroom doorway and showing distinctly lesbian tendencies, and the two tinted gentlemen were getting extremely overexcited by a very noisy singer on the TV. In fact, one way and another, the entire cast seemed to be making pretty heavy weather of it.

Now the black girl found herself being pursued in the street by a white-haired tramp in a dirty mac. Evidently he wasn't her type, although for my money it was a toss-up between him and the carrot. He was surprisingly nifty on his feet for one apparently so decrepit, but luckily the girl could shift a bit too, and in no time at all she was outside the house being comforted by the American who arrived at that moment, penniless, from the opposite direction.

In relief and gratitude, she took him up to her room and, while our two nancy boyfriends sat happily in a nearby pub watching a drag act, she made him a cup of coffee which she promptly poured into his crutch.

'Let me look,' she said. 'I'm a part-time nurse. A little massage is all that's needed.'

Would have thought that was the last thing that would have helped. And yet it certainly seemed to be doing wonders for both of them, and, as the American pointed out, 'It's not as scalded as all that.'

Could not resist glancing at the couple in front who appeared to have gone to sleep. Unless they, too, were up to no good. The man next door was tackling his third King Cone.

Meanwhile the lesbians were still fondling each other, the men had taken to biting each other's bottoms, and the massage had produced predictable results.

Decided the young couple in front definitely asleep.

Came the dawn and the milkman arrived, but no one was up earlier than this household (no joke intended), and by eight o'clock they were all hard at it again.

Later, they all went walking in the sunshine in Regent's Park.

Suddenly everything turned blue and they started to dream of who they would really like to be with. The black man fancied the carrot lady, Ilsa fancied the American, and the loo lady fancied the Japanese pansy.

Next, they were all in Hampton Court maze, bumping into each other and laughing and generally getting into a frightful muddle. In the end, though, they all ended up with the right partner and, because it was a nice day, they rushed off into the long grass and got busy.

Later, black and carrot got busy at home; ditto loo and Japanese on the roof.

Suddenly, for no apparent reason, they were all to be found sitting cross-legged in a circle on the grass without a stitch on, holding hands and kissing each other, while a choir sang 'All Together Now'.

And then the lights came up.

Rather regret now that I had not plumped for bill in

adjoining cinema: *Flesh Gordon* ('more laughs than lechery', – the *Guardian*) and *Deadly Weapons* starring the Incredible Chesty Morgan (72-32-36 – 'Seeing is believing. The outstanding attraction everyone is talking about.') Shall definitely have to make time for a return visit.

Home then by underground, convinced that everyone in the carriage knew where I had spent the afternoon.

Straight into a good hot bath followed by an individual steak and kidney pie and *Panorama*. I feel like a man who has just been let out of prison after a long stretch.

To bed early where I slept badly and dreamt constantly that Mrs Gurney from the flat downstairs was making a salad and chasing me round the kitchen with a huge carrot, and Miss Weedon from next door had unexpectedly developed the largest breasts in the world.

Tuesday

Had not in fact planned to resume my diary. However, can think of no better way of maintaining a day-to-day account of my researches. Not so much a diary perhaps as a writer's notebook along the lines of Maugham's.

Had barely got in this morning when the phone rang. It was Hugh Bryant-Fenn to say that my letter had arrived by the first post and that he would be delighted to give me all the assistance he could and what aspects of the subject particularly interested me.

I said, 'I realize you're not exactly a sexual athlete, Hugh, but . . .'

'I don't know who you think you are that you should make assumptions about other people's private lives with so much confidence and so little knowledge,' he said.

Was quite taken aback by this unexpected outburst. However, have not spent the last few months handling the firm's corporate image without developing an instinct for defusing awkward misunderstandings.

I said with a laugh, 'Come of it, Hugh. Knowing the sort of bloke you are. . .'

He said, 'How do you know what sort of bloke I am? Just because you once tagged on to me in Venice, that hardly entitles you to make value judgements on my sexual behaviour. I'll tell you one thing: the sort of man who allows his friend's budgerigar to die and then tries to cover up the fact by palming him off with a cheap double is not guaranteed to meet with great success with women.'

I said, 'I'm very sorry about the budgerigar, Hugh, but that's hardly the point.'

'On the contrary,' he said, 'it is very much the point. You doubtless see yourself as one of the world's great philanthropists, but the truth is you're as mean as all get out, and if there's one thing that women can't abide it's meanness.'

Pretty rich stuff coming from a man who's never once picked up a restaurant, hotel or airline bill in the last ten years.

I said, 'Hugh, for all I know you may be the world's greatest gift to women. Frankly, I could not give a row of beans one way or the other. It's quite obvious to me you have nothing useful to contribute towards this project, so let's just leave it at that, shall we?'

'Fine,' he replied. 'Your loss, not mine. Don't say I didn't offer.'

'I won't,' I said, and put the phone down on him. Looked up to find Sue standing in the doorway.

She said, 'I always think you can tell a lot about a man from the way he sounds on the phone.'

I said, 'Don't worry; I'm not always as bad tempered as this.'

'I don't mean you,' she said. 'I mean him.' She nodded towards the telephone.

'Who?' I said. 'Hugh?'

'Is that his name?' she asked. 'I only caught the Bryant-Fenn bit. I like the name Hugh. It's reassuring and manly. It reminds me of good tweed suits and lawns and labradors in front of a blazing log fire.'

'So you reckon Hugh's pretty hot stuff, do you?' I said.

She frowned. 'What a very vulgar expression,' she said. 'I merely said that, to judge from his voice, he sounded an attractive man.'

I laughed and said, 'You wouldn't say so if you saw him.'

'How do you know?' she said, and left the room, slamming the door behind her.

I enjoy the company of spirited women. The only drawback is that you never know from one minute to the next where you are with them.

On an impulse, rang Tim Pedalow. He's the sort of chap who knows the way the world wags, sexually speaking. He's always travelling here, there and everywhere on business, and no one's going to try to tell me he retires to his hotel room every evening after a quiet dinner and reads his Gideon Bible.

Despite the curiously open marriage they affect, Tim and Vanessa have always struck me as being a very physical couple, held together by a strong mutual interest in Sportsnight with C.

Tim said he was most interested to hear about my project. I said that I had always understood that he and Vanessa were confirmed hedonists.

'We were,' he said, 'until our last trip to California. Now we're confirmed disciples, and apostles, of the New Celibacy.'

I said that sounded a typical trans-Atlantic fad, if ever I'd heard one.

He said 'You may well laugh, but I can tell you, it's sweeping America and it's only a matter of time before it catches on over here.'

I said that I was very sorry but I wasn't quite sure what he was talking about.

He said, 'Don't be daft. You know very well what celibacy is. You've practised it enough yourself over the years. The retreat from sex was bound to happen on a huge scale sooner or later. It's the natural response to years of sexual overkill by people like Heffner and Guccione. It promotes an altogether higher and more everlasting sense of fulfilment.'

I replied that, following my own experiences in San Francisco, he could definitely count on my support in his new movement once I'd got my report out of the way.

He said, 'Yes, well, it's a greater sacrifice for some than for others.'

'You mean like Hugh Bryant-Fenn?' I said.

'Hugh?' he exclaimed. 'Don't be silly. He's the biggest ram this side of the Thames.'

I said, 'Hugh? A ram? Are you sure?'

'Ask any girl in London,' he exclaimed. 'You must have

heard of Hugh's famous big red book.'

Apparently Hugh is in the habit of recording in a large red notebook a blow by blow account of every encounter he enjoys with a member of the opposite sex.

'It must be a very slim volume,' I said,

'Don't you believe it,' said Tim. 'Poor old Theresa de Grande-Hauteville – Milne that was – once made the mistake of accepting an invitation from Hugh for dinner. He took her to some El Cheapo in Fulham, then back to his place for coffee. She popped into the loo to powder her nose and came back into the sitting room to find Hugh, stark naked, reclining on the chaise longue, smoking a large cigar and looking decidedly pleased with himself. As soon as she appeared, he sprang to his feet, sat her down with the red book with the words, "Why don't you have a look through this? I'll just see about the coffee," and tripped off into the kitchen. She waited till he was out of the room, nipped out into the hall, grabbed her coat and disappeared into the night.'

I said, 'But I saw them not so very long ago at your drinks party, chatting away as though nothing had happened.'

Tim said, 'As far as they're concerned, nothing did. That's why they're still friends.'

I said, 'Do you think Hugh might know anything about tarts, massage parlours, that sort of thing?'

'Probably,' he said. 'Why not ask him yourself?'

Tim Pedalow may be a lousy stockbroker, but I could almost forgive him the £420 he lost me a year ago for what he told me today.

Rang Hugh after lunch. Apologized for my irritable behaviour earlier and assured him that I had never for a moment doubted his expertise in the field of how's-your-father. I added that he had always been high on my list of experts to be interviewed, and suggested a good, long lunch (at my expense, of course) to chat things over.

He said, 'I knew you'd come round to it in the end. Unfortunately, I can't make lunch this week. I'm already committed to a couple for my column in *Bedroom* magazine.'

Made a mental note to quiz him about the men's magazine market.

He went on, 'And then, of course, on Friday I'm lunching with Sue.'

'Who's Sue?' I asked him.

He said, 'Your secretary, of course. Who else?'

'I never realized you knew my secretary,' I said.

'I don't,' he replied cheerfully. 'But we got on so well on the telephone and she has such a sexy voice that I suggested a meeting.'

I don't know why I should be so angry; she means nothing to me. But I am.

I said, 'Next week then?'

'You're on,' he said.

For some reason, am strongly reminded of those stories one used to read in the *News of the World* when one was at school – about dentists in the suburbs who gave their female patients gas and then took advantage of them. The really sexy ones were nearly always extremely unattractive. Things do not appear to have changed.

Thought about taking in a couple of hard-core porn shows on way home, but there was a rather good wildlife programme I wanted to see on BBC1 at 8.05. Besides, the vision of a naked Bryant-Fenn reclining on a chaise longue brandishing his confessions while my secretary busied herself in the kitchen was more than enough naked flesh to contemplate for one day.

Wildlife programme well up to BBC standards. Had not realized before that mute swans mated in that way, or that sex is so much a part of our lives without our realizing it. It's probably simply because I'm more sexually attuned than usual.

Wednesday

Walked into office this morning just as phone started ringing. Picked it up at once.

A man's voice said, 'Good morning, Miss Lovely Voice. Guess who?'

I said, 'Who exactly did you wish to speak to?'

'Is that you, Crisp?' the voice asked.

I said that it was.

'Oh, it's Hugh here. I thought you were somebody else.'

'Evidently,' I said.

He said, 'Actually it was you I wanted to speak to.'

He went on to explain that a friend of his was laying on a film show in Ashford, of all places, on Saturday night and would I like him to get me in on it?

I said, 'By an odd coincidence, I happen to be staying near Ashford for the weekend with my mother. What sort of film show?'

Hugh said, 'All I can tell you is that a friend of his has just made a film about W.B. Yeats which she hopes to sell to a television company. This is by way of being a sneak preview for a few close friends. It sounds just up your street.'

Why he should think this, I cannot imagine. However, have taken down particulars and said I'll look in if family commitments allow.

Hugh said, 'I think you'll find it'll be worth your while.' And he rang off.

Must confess to being rather intrigued. There has to be more to this than meets the eye, but what? May make the effort or may not. I'll see how I feel.

Must remember to ask Hugh if he knows Fiona Richmond. Shall have to think about buying a ticket for her latest show at the Whitehall, although it doesn't require a particularly fertile imagination to picture the sort of thing one is in for.

In many ways, am quite glad to be without a girlfriend for a while. I can imagine only too well what Jane would have had to say about my various outings. Strange how much I still miss having her around, though. It is some weeks now since we worked together on our abortive Young Conservative Dance and she announced she was engaged.

Which reminds me, I still haven't had a reply to my letter to Armitage. I am convinced there are several folds in the soft underbelly of the London entertainment scene in which he has dipped more than the occasional toe. Will try to ring him tomorrow.

Also nothing from Beddoes in Brussels.

To Soho again after lunch to make a serious start on the hard-core scene. Began my researches in Brewer Street. Wherever I looked my eye was dazzled by the neon lights of yet another sex-related premise, as I believe these places are known in official circles. Can hardly believe that I pass along these streets so often, yet apparently notice so little. But then, of course, one has better things to look out for from the back of a motorbike than thrusting breasts and provocative bottoms. So much for this so-called all-out porn war declared by the Conservatives on the Greater London Council.

Where is one to begin? The blurbs all promise so much. 'You'll never see anything sexier'; 'The latest in hard-core porno films'; 'All 100% hard-core porn. £3.50 for two-hour show'; 'All the best in hard-core from America, Denmark, Sweden, Great Britain, Germany'.

Hot Between the Legs, Country Bumkins, Up She Comes, Swedish Teenage Doll . . . What can they all be about? One hardly feels inclined to approach the oily-skinned scruffs who call out at one as one passes, and ask for a synopsis. To judge from my previous expedition into these foreign parts, 'Show now on, gents' is probably the only English phrase they know.

Am also slightly concerned about this business of club membership. Have not had a chance yet to check up on the legal ins and outs, but a voice somewhere at the back of my brain tells me that one has to wait twenty-four hours from the time of paying one's initial membership fee before one is officially a member. Or am I thinking of gambling clubs? At all events, would not care to be the innocent victim of some random police raid. Being the special case I am, I daresay one could persuade the authorities to keep one's name out of the papers, but there's always *Private Eye*. Not that Mother has ever subscribed to this excellent magazine, but I have a feeling Denys Ramsden's nephew takes it, and I wouldn't put it past him to go shooting his mouth off at a cocktail party. News travels fast in English villages.

Legal considerations apart, £3.50 seems a lot to shell out when, for only 50p, one can enjoy an equally rude experience in one's own private booth in the nearby Love Shop.

Changed a pound note at the desk and made my way into the gloomy interior, peering as I went at the titles pinned up on the doors. Very much torn between *Lay-By Lovers, Erotic Lesbians* and *Open for Anything*. Settled in the end, though, for *Gripped by Lust*. Not that this feeble tale of a burly judo instructor and his two attractive young female pupils gripped me – with lust or anything else.

Closed door, inserted coin and projector began to whirr. It soon became obvious from the grainy image flickering on the back of the door that, unfortunately, I had happened upon a very early instalment of the story.

After the burly instructor had watched the two girls throwing each other onto the floor, he sent one of them away for a shower and called the other back for some private tuition. To his surprise, she quickly had him flying through the air. He was obviously annoyed, if not aroused. Not that one could tell in those loose judo clothes.

Meanwhile, back in the dressing room, the less favoured girl was sitting in front of a mirror giving her neck and shoulders a bit of a rub. Before long, her hand had wandered unconsciously onto her bosoms and she was giving them a bit of a rub too. Then, before one knew what, she was giving every part of her body a good going over.

Meanwhile, back in the gym . . .

The money had run out.

Sat there for a while in the dark, wondering whether to change another pound. Things were obviously about to hot up, and very probably within the next 50p's worth. Decided to chance my arm and nipped out to desk. Slight delay owing to sudden arrival of a team of rowdy football supporters, rather the worse for wear. By the time I had transacted my business my booth was occupied.

I do not know which made me angrier: the fact that I would now never know who gripped who, or that someone else was even now enjoying the fruits of my extremely unsatisfying spadework.

Marched straight out without a second glance, across the road and into the Erotic 1 & 2 cinema complex. This was an altogether superior establishment, well-lit and welcoming. There was even a man washing the floor. Headed straight for booths. It's extraordinary to think that, only a couple of days ago, I would have been nervous and ill at ease entering a place like this, yet now I can walk in as easily and shamelessly as if I were about to see *Snow White and the Seven Dwarfs* at the Chelsea Odeon.

Choice of films considerably more attractive here. Finally chose one called *Rodox*. A suggestive if somewhat enigmatic title. I hoped I wasn't in for any corporal punishment.

Took my seat, inserted coin, but nothing happened. Pressed equivalent of Button A several times. Still nothing.

Made my way outside to glass booth to seek guidance. Inside, two men were watching a tennis tournament. Stan Smith was in action; I couldn't see who his opponent was. Would have given a lot to be at home watching the same thing with my feet up and a cup of tea and a couple of ginger biscuits at my side.

Explained my predicament re non-working of projector. One man looked round behind him where a stack of video cassette players were hard at work. Was reminded of a self-service garage. 'That's funny,' said the man. 'Should be okay.'

His colleague looked up briefly. The score, I could see, was deuce. 'Press the tit and stick your finger up the hole,' he said.

Returned to booth and sat there for several minutes, pondering advisability of following his bizarre instructions. Presumably he was referring to the small hole beneath the box where the money goes in. However, it has always been my policy in life never to stick my finger into anything unfamiliar and I was not about to start now. Anything could happen. Even electrocution. Worse still if I got my finger stuck and they had to send for the fire brigade to haul me out.

'Stick your finger up the wossit,' I heard the man calling outside the door.

The possibility then occurred to me that, by doing so, I might in some mysterious way enjoy a sexual thrill – electronically perhaps. Very gingerly I did as I had been told. There appeared to be nothing inside that would furnish me either with a sensation or my money back.

I returned to the booth. I hoped there wasn't going to be any trouble. These sort of people have a habit of turning ugly, I'm told, if they think a customer is trying to make monkeys out of them. However, they couldn't have been nicer and gave me another coin without a murmur. It's that sort of behaviour that makes one feel inclined to go back to

28

a place. In the circumstances, felt quite happy to ask them what the word MITTON meant on the bottom of every door sign.

'It's German,' one of them told me. '*Mit ton*. With sound.'

No whacking with sticks, I'm glad to report, but plenty of good old Rodox, provided by a man with a large moustache and a silly grin on his face, another with long hair and a permanently pained expression, and a blonde girl with an American accent.

Ton excellent. It certainly added to the whole thing no end, although there is a limit to the expressions of muttered ecstasy even the most articulate lover can dream up, and these three had definitely come to the end of theirs long before my 50p ran out.

Decided I owed it to the management to treat myself to another 50p's worth. Scouted round for a suitable sequel only to discover that all the booths were showing *Rodox*. Plucked up my courage to point out this fact to the man in the booth.

'Don't be a prat,' he said. 'That's the name of the effing distributor.'

Stan Smith seemed to be losing.

Place by now positively bustling with customers going about their business with all the dignity of men about to telephone their wives from Victoria Station to say there was a delay on the Oxted line and they'd be home a few minutes late.

Was feeling rather like a spot of lesbianism for a change, but unfortunately a small negro with a beard beat me to it, so settled on *Thai Tease* instead.

I don't know about Thai but a tease it certainly was. Not only was it a cartoon, but it appeared to have nothing whatever to do with the subject for which we were all gathered together under this unlikely roof. I do not believe I have ever been more disappointed over anything in my life. Thought I had probably pushed my luck quite far enough with the men in the booth, so left silently just as Stan Smith saved game point.

One way and another, as fascinating and educational an afternoon as I have spent in a long time.

Two points arise:

1. Is one to understand that there are many more women eager for a spot of straightforward, no-nonsense Sportsnight than one might think? If so, how is it that all the ones I ever meet seem to make such heavy weather of it?

2. 50p for a two-minute thrill is a good deal more expensive than may at first appear – especially for those of us old enough to remember the days of ten-shilling notes.

Interesting footnote: is it my imagination or am I suddenly quite keen at the prospect of a return visit? And, if so, should I be happy that I am throwing off my inhibitions, or alarmed at being so rapidly depraved?

To bed in thoughtful mood.

Thursday

Surprised and disappointed to have heard nothing still from Armitage. Obviously do not wish to give him the impression that I am running round after him, but must get on. Rang him immediately following a time-wasting Progress Report meeting on the Kellerman contract.

Apparently he had received my letter but just hadn't had time (or manners) to reply.

'I knew you'd call sooner or later,' he said.

I came straight to the point. 'You remember you once sent me to a massage parlour . . . ?'

'Vaguely,' he said. 'Why? Got a stiff neck again, have you? Or a stiff something else?' And he gave a vulgar guffaw.

I was in no mood for his style of crude innuendo and decided to knock the stuffing out of him straight away. 'Noel Annan,' I said, 'did not agree to be chairman of his distinguished commission because he had secret longings to be a radio interviewer, nor was Bernard Williams planning a career in obscenity.'

There was a pause and then Armitage said, 'So?'

I said, 'So . . . if I had wanted an excuse to patronize low haunts, I could have thought up an easier one than this.'

He said, 'So you're asking me to take you to some low haunts, is that it?'

'In a word,' I said, 'yes.'

'Massage parlours.'

'That depends,' I said.

'On what?' he said.

'Look, Armitage,' I said, 'I think I should tell you that I am perfectly capable of carrying out all the research necessary for this survey without anyone's help. I'm not some naive nincompoop, you know. I have been around.'

Armitage said, 'You don't have to justify yourself to me, old cock.'

I suppose I should not blame Armitage for trying to score off me. He has never properly recovered from losing his job to me as Assistant Group Head at Harley Preston last year, of course. However, cannot allow finer feelings to cloud one's judgement where business is concerned.

I said, 'Since we're on the subject, you wouldn't happen to know anything about contact magazines, would you?'

He said, 'Personally I have never felt the need to advertise for my pleasures. Why not try *Time Out*? Their lonely-hearts columns are full of that sort of thing.'

Having never subscribed to trendy way-out journalism, had always assumed *Time Out* to consist of nothing but long, serious reviews of lunchtime performances of incomprehensible left-wing plays in disused warehouses in Shoreditch, profiles of underground pop groups with silly names, and listings of demos by the Socialist Workers' Party. Was astonished upon buying my first copy, therefore, to discover that it is a perfectly straightforward guide to what's on in London. I cannot think how I can have survived all these years without it. It is obviously essential reading for anyone with the slightest interest in metropolitan life.

Turned to classified pages at back of magazine. I had no idea that so many young people experienced such difficulty in finding friends.

TALL, ATTRACTIVE, INTELLIGENT, FUN-LOVING CHAP, 24, enjoys T.S. Eliot, Astaire, Ayckbourn, drinking and eating – in or out. You are female, any age, quite tall, interesting. Photo.

AMUSING, INTELLIGENT BACHELOR, 37, wide tastes, own flat, car. Knows what's what. Seeks lively, attractive girl with eye to adventure. Photo/phone desirable.

HANDSOME STALLION seeks thoroughbred older mare with own cosy paddock.

Why men with so much to offer are not already fighting off women every minute of their lives I cannot think.

The women sound even less in need of an agony column.

BLONDE, TALL, SENSUOUS GIRL, 25 seeks well-educated, handsome, tall guy for fun evenings. No serious involvement.

ATTRACTIVE, INTELLIGENT BLONDE, 30, seeks loving, humorous, free-thinking male counterpart.

SENSUOUS CONTINENTAL LADY, 32, slim, intelligent, wide interests, seeks kind, good looking romantic male for wining and dining. Possibly more.

Cannot decide what is implied by phrases like 'fun-loving', 'possibly more', 'free-thinking' and so on. Are they a code for what I think they are? Or am I rapidly acquiring an over-developed sense of *double entendre*?

Feel my report requires a section on sex by advertisement, but how am I to present a true picture without personal experience? Am seriously considering putting in an ad myself and seeing what sort of replies I get. But would it be within my brief to follow up the most promising? Doubtless Hardacre thinks that, by leaving it to my own discretion, he has made things easier. In fact I am in even more of a muddle than ever. A restaurant critic can hardly describe the latest trattoria without first eating the food and drinking the wine and, as the late Kenneth Tynan once said (or was it Sheridan Morley?), the theatre critic's job is to tell his readers what it was like to be in a certain theatre on a certain night.

First things first though: I've devised a short advertisement along the lines quoted. I have rung the magazine in question and gather that, if I'm slippy about it, I will be just in time for next week's issue.

It reads:

ATTRACTIVE, SENSITIVE STALLION, 37. Fun-loving, adventurous, wide range of unusual tastes. Has been around a bit and knows the score. Seeks sophisticated, free-thinking, sensuous partner(s) for entertaining get-together, possibly more. Photo/phone please.

I do not think that leaves much room for doubt as to what I have in mind. If it brings in as large a response as I think it will, £14.90 will be little enough to add to my expenses chit.

Despite box number, am slightly concerned about putting my real name and address on the booking form. Just to be on the safe side, have given office address and an assumed name. Have a feeling this may be illegal, but no time to check now. Must make a note to inform post room that, if a package should arrive addressed to Mr John Ashford, it is for me.

Bryant-Fenn rang just before lunch and said he was calling to make sure I had Desmond's address for Saturday night and to check that I was still definitely coming.

I repeated that I would certainly try to make it, but that I could not guarantee that Mother had not committed me to some soirée or other in the village, in which case I was sure he would understand.

At this he became obviously agitated and said that he would not understand. The film show was to begin at nine sharp and if I could not make it I was to say so now.

I cannot imagine what all the fuss is about. However, rang Mother who said that, if I couldn't be bothered to come down for Christmas, it was perfectly obvious that I had no time for her or her circle and that I could keep my clever London friends as far as she was concerned. If I thought she had nothing better to do than waste time trying to integrate me into Kent society, then I had another think coming and would I be down in time on Saturday to pop into Ashford and pick up the cat's antibiotics from the vet, his surgery closed at noon, had I remembered?

Rang Hugh straight back and told him I was definitely on.

'Good,' he said. 'As long as I know who's coming. Will you be bringing anyone with you?'

I said that I didn't think Mother was that much of a Yeats fan but, if he wanted me to give someone a lift, I'd be happy to oblige.

'No, no,' he said. 'That's fine. Just as long as I know.'

Am beginning to wonder if all this eating out isn't beginning to turn his head.

To Soho again after lunch to complete my survey on

hard-core films. After much deliberation, decided to plump for hard-core club in Brewer Street which was showing a six-film programme consisting of *The Teenager, Surprise Orgy, Kinky Lips, Sex Fantasy, Date with Vanessa* and *Analitis*, which I always thought was the name of a haemorrhoid cream.

'Two fifty, squire,' said the man at the box office. The fact that he was English I found strangely reassuring. Thought I ought to come clean straight away and confess that I was not actually a member.

'Don't you worry about that, my son,' said the man. 'Straight through the doors and down the stairs.'

Picked my way down steep, narrow staircase and into tiny, smoke-filled room. The film clattered scratchily through a glass panel at the back and on to a pocket handkerchief-sized screen.

Nearly all three rows of seats occupied by silent staring customers but managed to squeeze on to end of back row, took out my notebook and prepared for the worst. I cannot say that I was disappointed.

Goodness knows which of the films was which. Only one, which was faintly Germanic, actually had a story and dialogue. It concerned a virginal young blonde and her wicked auntie who ran a brothel – with the inevitable results.

The other five claimed no such pretensions to dramatic art. They consisted merely of men Sportsnighting with women in a number of different positions to the accompaniment of moans, groans and muttered imprecations.

I'm surprised the man next to me managed to sleep so soundly throughout with all that noise going on.

Was quite unable to doze off myself and was forced to sit there in the dark staring expressionlessly up at the screen like my fellow voyeurs while yet another moustachioed ex-lorry driver struggled undecorously out of his underpants and socks on the Dralon in somebody's front room in Ealing and braced himself to meet the onslaught of yet another uninviting crutch.

The female anatomy has never had my vote as Aesthetic Object of the Year at the best of times, and nothing that I saw this afternoon has persuaded me to change my mind. I had no idea cameras could zoom in as close on anything as they did on those gaping wounds. Had the man next to me woken up suddenly and looked up at the screen he might have been forgiven for thinking that he had arrived in the middle of an episode of *Your Life in their Hands*.

From the titillation point of view, they rated somewhere between a half and one out of ten on my personal scoreboard. On the other hand, as sex education films, showing what goes where and how, they could hardly be bettered.

As far as the performers went (generally too far), I do not believe I have seen so many unattractive people captured for posterity on celluloid in one afternoon. I am told on quite good authority that many of the people who take part in rude films are out-of-work actors. If so, I can perfectly see why.

Friday

Devoted morning to penning a memo to Hardacre in anticipation of his return on Monday morning. Unable to dictate, however, as Sue did not deign to roll in until nearly eleven, airily announcing by way of excuse that she had been to the hairdresser. Hoped it was not for Bryant-Fenn's benefit, but did not like to ask. Is it my imagination or am I slightly jealous?

Left rough draft of memo on her desk and took an early lunch myself.

On way back to office, popped into local newsagent to buy evening paper. Noticed one of the popular dailies was carrying a story on the proliferation of strip clubs in the Midlands – graphically illustrated, to judge from the extremely well-endowed performer on the front page. Could not resist commenting on this to sour-faced woman behind counter.

The woman being served in front of me said, 'They'll do anything to sell papers these days.'

'Bloody disgusting, if you ask me,' said the shopkeeper. 'Printing that sort of stuff with kiddies around.'

'Too right,' said the other woman. 'And they wonder why the youth of Britain is depraved.'

'You see articles about it in the papers,' said the shopkeeper.

'Yer,' said the other. 'In papers like these, more than likely.'

'Bloody disgraceful,' agreed the shopkeeper.

Bought my paper, turned and found myself face to face with a revolving rack jammed solid with glossy men's magazines – *Penthouse, Men Only, Mayfair, Knave, Whitehouse, Romp, International Model Directory, Escort*, and many more. Funnily enough, have been thinking that sooner or later I must get in a supply of these for research purposes. Picked up special Caligula issue of *Penthouse* for idle flick through.

The woman behind the counter said, 'No use trying to do that. I've stuck them all up with sellotape.'

I said with an ironic laugh, 'Yes, well, you wouldn't want kiddies seeing this sort of thing, would you?'

She lit a cigarette and coughed horribly. 'It's not that,' she croaked. 'It's to stop dirty sods like you coming in here, picking them out, having a quick flip through and putting them back again.'

I said cheerfully, 'Well, you certainly succeeded in my case,' and made to put the magazine back. Unfortunately, the rack was so full that I had to force the thing in and, in doing so, slightly tore the front cover.

'You'll have to buy it now, won't you?' said the woman, coughing. Had no alternative but to pay up.

I said pointedly, nodding towards the offending newspaper, 'A slight case of double standards, wouldn't you say?'

She stubbed out her cigarette and put her hands on her hips. 'I've nothing against sex,' she said. 'In its proper place.'

Suddenly noticed a small cardboard box on the counter containing a number of copies of something called *The Sex Maniac's Diary*. It looked rather fun and only £2.75.

I said, 'I'll have one of those.'

'I thought you would,' she said.

Have made a note to include a section on sex among the middle-aged.

Saturday

To Kent soon after breakfast. Mother still going on about

Christmas, despite my making special detour to collect cat's medicine – and paying for it.

A cold, damp day, so spent most of afternoon in front of TV watching the rugger international followed by wrestling. Am wondering if I should include a section on sex in sport? Had always understood women not generally excited by the sight of the male nude body and, if Sue's experience is anything to go by, they never buy male pinup magazines. Yet I have never seen women work up such a head of steam over anything as that front row did in the Fairfields Hall, Croydon, at the sight of 'Flash' Gordon sorting out 'Pretty Boy' Cartwright over three rounds. I'm surprised the Soho pornographers have not thought of adding an extra booth specializing in male wrestling for female customers. There'd be a fortune in it. Fortunately, Mother so engrossed in cat's gippy tummy that I was not called upon to explain my present occupation.

After supper I announced that I had to go into Ashford for a bit.

She said, 'But aren't you going to watch *Dallas*? I thought you liked *Dallas*. That's why I got supper ready early, so that you could watch *Dallas*.'

Told her not to wait up for me, but I knew she would anyway.

Had rather more difficulty finding Hugh's friend's house than had anticipated. For some reason, had not imagined that anyone he knew would live in quite such a suburban street. Met at the door by Desmond's wife, Anthea, a pale, skinny girl with lank fair hair and slightly protruding teeth. Surprised to hear I was the first arrival, even though it was already nearly 8.45.

Anthea took my anorak and led me through to the sitting room. Floral patterned carpet and striped Regency wallpaper. At one end a small screen had been erected. Ashtrays and bowls of crisps and peanuts had been placed at strategic intervals. A projector was propped up on a small table, beside which a burly, balding man with a heavy moustache was mending a plug.

'Desmond,' I cried, striding forward with arm outstretched. 'Thank you so much for asking me. My name's Crisp.'

'Actually,' said Anthea, 'this is Ray, from the local

garage. He's very kindly lent us his projector and agreed to show the films.'

Ray nodded at me in an offhand manner. He didn't look the Yeats type to me.

After a couple of minutes, Desmond himself arrived. He was about my age, on the short side, with a mass of shaggy black hair. His T-shirt had OXFORD UNIVERSITY written across it.

'Aha,' I said, 'another Oxford man, I see. Which college were you?'

'I wasn't,' he said. 'I bought it in a secondhand shop in Canterbury.'

We then went through to the next room where French bread and cheese and pâté and two-litre bottles of Valpolicella and large cans of Ruddles had been laid out on the dining room table.

Desmond poured us all a glass of wine and said, 'Are you new to this sort of thing?'

'Oh no,' I said. 'We quite often have parties like this in London.'

'Oh, that's all right then,' he said. 'Only Hugh did mention something about you needing a bit of persuasion, shall we say?'

At that moment the doorbell went and suddenly the room was full of people, laughing and kissing and shrieking at the tops of their voices.

Desmond tried to introduce me to them all, but the only names I caught were those of Lady Somebody-or-other and her daughter who, I gathered, was the director of the film. They had brought with them a silent young man with very close-cropped hair and a ring through one ear, and someone I took to be his girlfriend. Also a scruffy blonde woman and her husband who was tall and thin with glasses and a beard. They hailed apparently from New Zealand. I said that I had always wanted to go to New Zealand, to which the woman replied that she couldn't think why anyone should want to go there. She had spent her entire life trying to get away. In my experience, it never pays to try to make conversation with disgruntled colonials.

A minute or two later, there was another ring and Hugh appeared, looking foolish in jeans and leather jacket, with a flimsy silk scarf round his neck held by a little gold ring. If there's one thing I can't bear it's people who aim low, sartorially speaking, and miss. I felt quite embarrassed – though not half as much as I was when I saw that the girl clutching his arm was none other than my secretary, Sue.

Naturally I kept my surprise to myself and behaved as I would with any old friend. I even kissed Sue on both cheeks. Bang go my chances of getting another letter decently typed, I daresay.

Made mistake, as I always do, of asking Hugh what he was up to, whereupon he launched into a long and detailed account of his latest curriculum vitae. Not only has he been asked, in his capacity as Wig and Hairpiece Editor of *Barbershop Quarterly*, to undertake a six-week lecture tour next autumn in the Far East on the subject of The Toupée and its Place in the Developing World, but he is to be the chairman, if you please, of a new TV quiz show about food and wine called *Pass the Port*. He tried to explain the rules to me but I simply couldn't make head or tail of it – nor did I wish to. Sue, I'm sorry to say, seemed to be taken in by the whole thing. I'm beginning to have second thoughts about her. Soon everyone was tucking into the French bread and Valpolicella, and by the time we all adjourned to the sitting room, one or two were in a very merry mood indeed.

As Anthea was turning out the lights, Bryant-Fenn whispered to me, 'Never mind, it'll make good copy for you.'

The first thing to appear on the screen was a dealer film for Skoda cars. While I was mildly interested to learn of the vehicle's good roadholding and low fuel consumption, the connection between the Czechoslovakian motorcar industry and William Butler Yeats completely eluded me. Could only assume this was the price Mr and Mrs Desmond had to pay in return for Ray's services for the evening. There was a short break while the garage man laced up the next film and we settled back to twenty minutes of unrelieved boredom while someone with an Irish accent intoned line after line of lugubrious verse over endless shots of rain-swept countryside.

The sigh of relief that went up simultaneously with the lights was only too audible. Frankly, I have always suspected Yeats of being an overrated poet and am now more convinced of it than ever.

And then the most astonishing thing happened. The lights went down, the projector whirred once more into life, and on the screen appeared the vision of two people deeply embroiled in as steamy a session of Sportsnight with C as you could wish to see.

I could not believe my eyes. Obviously, by an astounding stroke of luck, I had fallen upon one of those groups of blue movie enthusiasts one reads about in certain Sunday newspapers. The story was as insubstantial, the inquisitiveness of the camera as intrusive and the physical appearance of the two protagonists every bit as unattractive as I'd remembered from my afternoon at the ciné club. The only difference was that, while those films had been flecked throughout with the scratches of a thousand showings, this one was blurred and contorted by strange colours, wispy gauzes and sudden flashes of bright lights.

On and on it ground. Once someone coughed gently, but apart from that and the whirring of the projector the whole spectacle took place in total silence. But all bad things must come to an end, and with one final leap and judder, the couple concluded their bizarre performance.

Had assumed that everyone would get to their feet, make muttered excuses and leave as quickly as possible. Far from it. There they all sat, chatting politely with one another and discussing the finer points of the film as calmly as if they had just sat through *The Seventh Seal*. Suddenly the scruffy New Zealand woman stood up and made her way to the front.

'If any of you have any questions, I'd be glad to answer them,' she said.

Suddenly realized to my astonishment that this was the woman in the film. Not only that, but she had also directed it. Or rather, as she put it so graphically, 'set the camera and us in motion'. To add to the confusion, the bearded man she had come with and who I had understood to be her husband, was not the man in the film.

She blithely explained that all the funny marks on the film were specially made by herself during processing, with paint, with silver strips, and with tiny feathers. 'I wanted this to be the first ever truly *art* blue movie,' she explained.

Everyone, it seemed, was bursting to ask her something – even Lady Thing, who piped up, 'Wasn't it rather difficult ensuring the camera was pointing at the right place?'

'It was all right,' answered the New Zealander, 'as long as we didn't kick it over.'

Everybody roared. As I was leaving, could not resist buttonholing Desmond. 'Is there much of this sort of thing going on round here?' I asked him.

'Much of what sort of thing?' he asked.

'Well,' I said, 'you know, blue movie clubs and so on.'

'I don't know what you mean,' he said. 'We happen to be the Ashford Branch of the W.B. Yeats Appreciation Society, and if you came for any other reason, then I am only sorry Hugh asked you.'

And he closed the door on me.

I give up. Am I going sex mad or what?

Home for an early night with a hot-water bottle and a glass of warm milk, only to find Mother still glued to *Parkinson*.

'Why aren't you on this sort of programme?' she asked.

'Because I'm not famous enough,' I answered.

'That's no excuse,' she said. 'Neither was Michael Parkinson till he got on and now look at him.'

Could not bring myself to reply.

Sunday

Woken at nine by Mother with a cup of tea and the news that the weather was, if anything, worse than yesterday but that bright periods were expected, moving slowly into the east by late afternoon.

'By which time,' I said, 'it will be dark and I will be gone.'

'There's no pleasing you sometimes,' she said. 'I blame it on the sort of life you live in London.'

'What sort of life?' I said.

She said, 'Well, since you've brought up the subject, I might as well tell you that when I rang your office last Thursday to find out what time you'd be down, whoever it was who answered the phone said you'd gone to Soho and were not expected back.'

'Well?' I said. 'I expect I'd gone there to lunch.'

'At four o'clock in the afternoon?' she said, and left the room.

Thank heavens she did not find my *Sex Maniac's Diary*. I wouldn't put it past her to go through my things while I'm out. Even my sock drawer.

Had not had a chance to look through it myself until today. Waited till she had gone to Sung Eucharist and settled down to it over coffee and biscuits.

The first thirty or so pages are packed with fascinating information for those who make a hobby of hanky-panky in all its shapes and forms. There's a Good Orgy Guide containing addresses in France, Germany, the United States and Australia, though not, I'm sorry to say, in Great Britain. A pity, since this is an area that will obviously need looking into.

Am quite amused by the Catalogue of Sex Games ('some traditional, some standard, some rarely attempted'), although I suspect that, if someone suggested Guess the Length of My Husband to me by way of an icebreaker at a party, I might easily be tempted to make an excuse and leave. That way I could be sure of avoiding such later delights as Ready, Steady, Gonads, Pantie Pickin' and the Eurovision Prong Contest.

I cannot think of an occasion off-hand when the phrase *Je suis masochiste; j'ai besoin d'un(e) sadique* would spring readily to the lips, but a list of foreign phrases of a sexual nature could certainly prove useful to one or two people I know.

The most interesting section of all for me is the one entitled Source Guide to the Best Sex in the World. Here, listed alphabetically, is all the information the most enthusiastic connoisseur of how's-your-father could possibly need.

Am fascinated to learn that the Messila Beach Hotel in Kuwait is highly recommended for women on the lookout for frustrated men, and that the Los Gatos Lodge in California is so full of loose women that there is a permanent queue ten yards long of men waiting to get in. I do not imagine that I will be in the area again myself in the very near future, but if ever I am and I'm at a loose end, I shall certainly try to get along.

Cannot make up my mind whether I am amused by the diary or shocked. My instinct is to put it away in a drawer and forget about it. On the other hand, I do need a pocket diary, thanks to the tight-fistedness of my so-called business friends, and if anyone were to comment on my curious choice, I could always laugh it off as a joke.

Except with Mother, of course.

Monday, 29 January

Memo

To: Keith Hardacre
From: Simon Crisp   29 January

Re: *The Crisp Report*

Welcome back! Just to let you know how things are going on the above front.

Have already completed sex film section and am due to tackle sex shops very shortly. Also have various irons in the fire re massage parlours, orgies, wife swapping, etc.

A couple of quick ones: am still a little vague about this tricky problem of *first-hand* research. It's one thing to sit through a pornographic film, but massage parlours and brothels raise quite different moral points. Also expenses. Shall obviously have to interview one or two people over lunch. Would not wish Barfords to be shown up in a mean light.

Do you by any chance know, or know anyone who knows, Fiona Richmond?

S.C.

Beddoes rang in the afternoon to say that he will be coming over on February 14th. Am not sure whether to read anything into choice of date or not. At all events, he says he will be delighted to provide me with a crash course on London after dark.

Could not resist saying that I hoped it would involve rather more than cruising up and down the red-light district waving at girls through the car window, which had been the high spot of my recent visit to Brussels.

He said, 'That depends who's picking up the tab,' and emitted one of those suggestive laughs that helped make sharing a flat with him such a misery.

Am already beginning to wonder if I was wise to bring him into this. Frankly, the sooner Hardacre comes back with a firm answer about expenses, the happier I shall be. Why is it that some people cost you money as soon as look at you?

No sign of Sue all day. I can see I'm definitely going to have to read the riot act to that young lady.

Tuesday

Rang Hugh first thing to thank him for Saturday evening.

He said, 'Pity you had to rush away like that. It developed into a very interesting evening.'

I said, 'Unfortunately, I do not share your friends' passion for Yeats.'

'What's Yeats got to do with it?' he said, and chuckled knowingly.

The trouble with people whose lives are continually directed by PROs is that they get into such a habit of talking in riddles that in the end one can't even ask them the time of day without the help of an interpreter.

Felt sure he was trying to tell me that, as a result of the blue movie, someone overstepped the mark. I came straight to the point. 'You don't mean an o-r-g-y, by any chance, do you?' I asked him.

'I don't know what you're talking about,' he replied. 'Ray showed us the films he'd shot on holiday in Peru, that's all. No o-r-g-i-e-s in that, as far as I can remember. A lot of Inca ruins though. And llamas. Jolly enterprising for a local garage man, I'd say. Wouldn't mind having a look at South America myself one day. Another string to my bow. Take a few snaps, work up a few stories, it'd be a sure-fire hit on the luncheon club circuit. Seventy-five quid a time, first class rail fare, free nosh, no trouble. I'll have to see someone at an airline about fixing up a freebie.'

I said, 'I should be glad if you would explain how it is that, if everyone at Ashford is as innocent as you claim, we sat through fifteen minutes of the most blatant pornography I have ever witnessed.'

Hugh said, 'Oh that. We always have to put up with one of those when we meet at Desmond's. Ray has a penchant for that sort of thing and, unless we allow him to run one or two, he sulks and won't lend us the projector.'

I said, 'But I thought the film had been made by that blonde New Zealand girl.'

'So it was,' said Hugh.

I said, 'But I understood her to be a friend of Lady Thing's daughter.'

Hugh said, 'There are some people in this life who are perpetually adding two and two together and making five.' And he rang off.

Heavens knows what it's all about. No one else seems to.

Sue deigned to roll in shortly after ten.

'Good afternoon,' I said. 'And where were you all yesterday?'

'Round and about,' she said. 'Doing things for Mr Pratt mainly.'

'Like what, for example?' I said.

'Oh,' she said, waving an airy arm, 'you know – the usual sort of things one does: taking dictation, typing up minutes of meetings, booking restaurants, having lunch.'

I said, 'But what are you doing working for Pratt? You're meant to be *my* secretary.'

She said, 'Oh I met him on the way in and he asked me if I was very busy, and I said no, you were out most of the time anyway, and he said could I spare a moment to help him out as his secretary is away ill. Personnel hadn't been able to rustle him up a temp at short notice.'

I said, 'But this is disgraceful. Why didn't someone have the common courtesy to come and say something to me?'

Sue said, 'I assumed Neville had.'

Rang Neville at once and made my feelings known in no uncertain terms.

He said, 'Sorry, old man. I thought it had all been fixed up between you and Keith.'

Immediately rang Keith who was in Stockholm again, according to Miss Hippo. Apparently he sent me a memo yesterday afternoon. I said that I had certainly received no communication of any sort along those lines. She said she was sure she had sent it and that was that.

Shortly before lunch, one of the spottier messenger boys stuck his head round the door and said, 'Mr Mann?'

I told him he must have got the wrong office.

'Funny,' he said. 'Says here Room 302, Mr D.O. Mann.'

I said, 'You'd better let me look at that,' whereupon the boy rushed across the room, threw the envelope on the desk and rushed out again, wearing the stupidest grin I've ever seen.

Opened envelope to find Keith's memo. On looking more closely at envelope, realized that someone had not only pasted a thin strip of paper over my name and written the false name on top, but that 'Man' did not have two n's as I had at first assumed.

I detect the hand of the post room in this somewhere. Could kick up a stink, but have decided it's probably better to do nothing. Those who undertake work of this nature must expect a certain amount of scorn and abuse. If Lord Longford could put up with it and retain his dignity, so can I.

Memo

To: Simon Crisp
From: Keith Hardacre   29 January

Thank you for your note. Unfortunately, am just off to Sweden for a four-day conference so am unable to deal with your queries for the moment. Can you wait until next week? In the meantime, feel you should be hurrying things along a bit. You haven't gone quite as far into the subject as I'd hoped.

R. Hippo
Dictated by Mr Hardacre and signed in his absence.

Considering the effect a report of this kind is bound to have on the corporate image of Barfords both here and abroad, feel I am not commanding the respect I should.

Wednesday

On reflection, am quite relieved Sue has been taken off my hands for a bit. I really don't have enough work for her here. More importantly, despite her unfortunate liaison with Bryant-Fenn, feel we could definitely make music together, given the right circumstances, and those do not include working closely together in an atmosphere of blatant sexuality.

In my experience, sex should be kept under wraps, like a Christmas present, if it is to work at a personal level, and to be discussing the subject all day long is enough to put anyone off the whole thing for good.

A more pressing problem, however, is how I should proceed re adultery. Am certainly not prepared to break a Commandment for the sake of mere sociology, nor can I think of anyone with whom I could possibly arrange to do so in the short time at my disposal.

May have to resort to a marriage guidance counsellor.

Friday

Great excitement. Today's the day my ad came out in *Time Out*. Hurried early to newsagent to be sure of getting a copy.

Turned to back pages and for a moment could not spot it at all. Realize now I should have gone for semi-display, as the girl had suggested. The wording certainly has the right feeling of sophisticated know-how, but will anyone ever find it?

Suddenly realized to my horror that, in my effort to keep the cost down, had completely failed to specify gender of sensuous partner(s) being sought. Does this mean I can expect a mailbag filled with strange requests from gay guys? Or, an even more alarming prospect, bi-guys?

I hope this is not going to end in tears.

Saturday

To Whitehall Theatre in the evening to see Fiona Richmond in her latest sex comedy. Decided to take pot luck and arrived a few minutes before curtain-up.

Interested to note that, while rest of West End theatre is struggling to attract audiences, Miss Richmond appears to be pulling them in in their hundreds. In fact, had quite a job getting a decent seat at all. Seriously toyed with idea of telling them who I was, but would not have wanted the news that a writer was out front to filter backstage. I know how these things can affect performances.

Audience in lively mood. Had distinct impression most of them had come straight on from the pub. At all events they were in good voice – especially a couple in my row.

Had certainly expected an evening of skimpy swimwear and possibly the occasional fleeting glimpse of a bosom or two, but was not prepared for the half dozen naked girls who strolled on to the stage in the first few minutes. The two men in my row, however, were evidently very much at home.

'Get 'em off,' came the shout the moment the girls appeared.

Scarcely a scene took place from then on in which they did not participate verbally from the dress circle.

'Someone's coming,' cried one of the girls at one point, looking anxiously into the wings. 'It's a man.'

'Not me, darling,' shouted one of the jokers.

Jokes of course depend very much on the sort of mood one is in, and I'm afraid that, when one is wearing one's reporter's hat, one cannot expect to join in the roars of laughter with quite the gay abandon displayed by the rest of the audience.

In the circumstances, was relieved not to be in the front row of the stalls and thus a butt for the comedian's saucy repartee. 'Enjoying it, sir? Yes, I can see you are. Sticks out a mile,' etc.

Fiona Richmond certainly lived up to her reputation as Britain's Number One Sex Symbol in every sense of the word. She has a wonderfully warm personality and a magnificent figure, which she shows off to advantage at every possible opportunity. It's hard to believe she's a vicar's daughter. Yet a friend of Tim Pedalow's cousin knew someone who was married by her father. Either that or prepared for confirmation.

In the interval, strolled round the foyer and bars, making mental sociological thumbnail sketches of members of the audience. While one was a million miles from Alan Bennett country in purely audience terms, in terms of the characters he portrays, there was a rich vein of comic raw material here which Alan could certainly tap to his advantage. In fact, might seriously consider dropping him a note along those lines. I think he'd appreciate it. As a writer, I know I would.

On way from loo, noticed a door marked PRIVATE. CHARGING ROOM. Is this where particularly rowdy customers are taken when things get out of hand, one wonders?

Curious how in second half of show one scarcely noticed nudity and rude language. In fact, characters with clothes on seemed positively out of place. I imagine one gains the same impression after one has been in a nudist colony for a few days. Perhaps I should see for myself. Am always being accused of being too inhibited. A bit of good, honest, down-to-earth sun worshipping might help me to be more carefree with my body.

After the show, on an impulse, went to the stage door and asked to see Miss Richmond.

I am not one of these trendy theatre goers who will insist on 'going round', as they say in theatrical circles, on the thinnest pretext and hobnobbing with the actors. And although the connection through Tim's cousin's friend might seem to many rather too vague for comfort, felt myself duty-bound, as a fellow student of the sexual scene, to introduce myself.

Explained who I was to the doorkeeper who passed the information on to the star by telephone. Finally he told me that she would see me briefly, but that she had a dinner engagement and would I mind waiting a moment or two while she had a shower. Someone would be down to fetch me.

Could hardly believe my good fortune. At the same time, I was as nervous as a schoolboy on his first date.

After a while, a young man appeared and escorted me upstairs in the lift. I said, 'Does Miss Richmond have many journalists coming to see her?'

'Search me, mate,' he said. 'I'm only a stagehand round here, not a bleeding press agent.'

Fiona's dressing room occupied by a young man

lounging on a settee drinking a glass of red wine.

'Help yourself,' he said, indicating the bottle.

Wondered if he was her dinner date.

Having read one of her pieces in an old copy of Armitage's *Men Only*, in which she 'road-tested' different men, reckoned he was in for a pretty lively evening. Frankly he looked a bit frail for the task to my way of thinking.

Fiona arrived, fresh from her shower. She is smaller than I imagined but none-the-less attractive for that. Unable to comment on her figure owing to towelling dressing gown pulled tightly around her. However, the bone structure of face quite superb.

Unfortunately, she made no attempt to introduce me to her friend. However, flattered and surprised to discover she knew my name. Could not resist commenting on the fact and said that I had not realized my reputation had spread quite so far.

'Actually,' she said, 'the stage doorkeeper just rang and told me.'

We chatted idly for a minute or two about the show. Not wishing to appear too sycophantic, I said that I had been a keen theatre goer for many years and had even at one time contemplated treading the boards myself, following critical acclaim for my performance as the Earl of Surrey in a college production of *The Shoemaker's Holiday* at Oxford, but I was something of a novice when it came to live sex shows. Was going on to explain my views on censorship when she cut me short by pointing out that she considered the expression 'sex show' to be damning with faint praise. It had in fact been adapted from a comedy written by a well-known French dramatist and, as such, was no different from many other West End successes.

This was fascinating stuff. I've often heard it said that there is a great deal more to Fiona than just a beautiful body and there was no doubt in my mind that on the evidence of her conversation so far I was dealing with a keen and original mind.

Surprised to discover as I walked back to the car that I was actually quite jealous of her dinner date. Also that the car had been towed away for being parked on a double yellow line.

This meant my having to take a taxi down to the Kennington Car Pound, wait around for an age while the man on duty finished his cup of tea and filled out various forms etc., and then take another taxi home because I had stupidly forgotten to come out with any money and was thus unable to pay the £29 fine.

An irritating, depressing and expensive end to an otherwise fascinating day.

On the credit side, have agreed with Fiona that I will call her in the week to arrange a proper interview, and can probably swing the fine on expenses. Assuming I have a proper expense account, that is.

Monday, 5 February

The start of the Sex Shop Week and the day on which I expect to receive a definite answer from Hardacre re expenses, etc.

Decided to begin at shop I once visited last year to buy sex manual for Jane. Am still slightly baffled as to why a place like that should carry books on car maintenance as an aid to relieving tension. On the other hand, anyone could be forgiven for believing that Auto-Therapy was about something quite different.

Doubtless Jane passed it on to Armitage when she went to live with him in his converted workman's dwelling in Camberwell. I can think of no better outlet for his over-developed sexuality than the Natchford Special he was always on about.

Shop every bit as crowded with shifty-looking browsers as I remember it. As a comparatively old hand, found myself entering with a jauntiness that was certainly lacking the last time I crossed this particular threshold.

Began on ground floor. Would not have believed it was possible to think up so many ways of increasing one's enjoyment of Sportsnight with Coleman. Naturally, as a man, am extremely sympathetic towards anyone who experiences difficulty in getting himself geared up for a session. However, the day I have to rely upon a tube of Erector Prompt for a spot of hanky-panky I'll seriously consider going into a monastery.

Assuming one has set things in motion, as it were, the next thing one has to worry about is keeping it all going.

51

Hence the huge stocks of sprays specially designed to stop you getting overexcited too early and thus mucking up the whole thing for all concerned.

One in particular, called Stud, seems to be more successful than most – so much so that they even offer free brochures telling you all about the product. It comes in a tiny gold and white aerosol can, about the size of those things people use to conceal their bad breath, and is apparently 'unchallenged throughout the world for quality, effectiveness and satisfaction in reducing oversensitivity'.

All you do is, about five minutes before you think Sportsnighting is about to reach a serious stage, whip out your tiny tube and give your weasel three or four quick squirts. Quite what the effect of this is I can only guess. Presume it makes everything numb, in which case I'd imagine the whole object of the exercise is largely negated anyway. There is, of course, the added danger that the well-equipped ladies' man might forget which tube is which and, following a garlicky meal, give his mouth a quick one-two and be unable to taste a thing for the next fortnight.

For those who suffer from the opposite problem there are Erotic Explosion Creams and Orgasm Boosters.

Weasel enlargers are evidently another popular line these days. The treatment, as far as one can gather, involves a transparent plastic tube and a small hand pump. Quite how this has the desired effect is difficult to see without actually spending £9.95 and finding out for oneself. Frankly I think Barfords have better things to do with their money in these hard times than waste it on increasing the size of their executives' weasels.

On the other hand, for a mere £7.75 it is possible – if the blurb on the box is to be believed – to create the illusion of magnitude with the use of a simple device known as The Butch Harness. By all accounts it will maintain 'the fullness and allure of the slight erection, particularly when worn with jeans or tight trousers'.

Was most intrigued. Is it really possible to go round for hours on end with a slight you-know-what and, if so, is such a physical condition really guaranteed to have women going weak at the knees?

Decided I had pussyfooted around for long enough. The

time had come to put the whole issue to the test. Luckily, the box fits neatly into one's overcoat pocket.

Decided against a talking blow-up rubber lady ('Designed by a man who wants her as much as you do, she is ever eager, every ready and never says no. Comes complete with underwear set and vibratory control'); ditto a pair of Dancing Bullets, said to be 'an exquisite pleasure source known to the ancients'. (Am not sure whether this refers to the Greeks and Romans etc. or OAPs.)

Interested to note how few women one sees in sex shops. *Tant mieux* for all our sakes.

Re rubberwear, leather underpants, plastic macs etc., I'm afraid it all leaves me rather cold. However, may well return to this subject at a later date.

To the magazine section next for a browse. These fall roughly into three categories:

a) The good old standbys – *Penthouse*, *Mayfair*, *Men Only*, *Rustler*, etc.
b) The ones that give the impression of being saucier because they are wrapped in cellophane and cost five times as much.
c) The ones that cater for those with an eye to curious physical deformities – e.g. *Bounce: Real Life Experiences of Big-Breasted Women*, *Superdong*, and *Bra Busters* – all featuring men and women beside whom the Elephant Man would have appeared positively normal.

Had in fact been planning to do my survey of the men's magazine market at a later date, but decided to hurry things along a bit by buying a small selection of the more popular range straight away – *Whitehouse*, *Knave* and *Men Only* to add to my Caligula edition of *Penthouse*.

Luckily there was a newspaper stand right outside the shop so that I was able to carry my purchases home concealed in a copy of the *Radio Times*.

Paused for a last look at lighted window. Was slightly puzzled by a couple of large gold balls hanging by a string which I hadn't noticed before. Stared at them for a long time but quite unable to guess their possible function.

Felt it was only my duty to pop back and get to the

bottom of the mystery. 'Excuse me,' I said *sotto voce*, to assistant, 'but can you possibly tell me what those gold balls in the window are for?'

'They're Christmas decorations,' he said. 'I've been meaning to take them down for weeks.'

Would have to pick on someone with a particularly penetrating voice.

On way out again, who should I bump into but Philippe de Grande-Hauteville, of all people.

When I explained that I was doing some very interesting research, he said, 'For the BBC, I suppose?'

If I've told him once, I've told him a dozen times that I do not work for the Corporation, but it's like talking to a brick wall. Either he's very much stupider than everyone takes him for, or else he could do with a refresher course in conversational English.

A far greater worry, though, is that he is bound to mention our meeting to Theresa and, knowing what a gossip she is, it will be round all my friends, including Jane, in no time. I see no alternative but to ring them all up and explain the situation before she has had a chance to get on the phone. But I'm going to have to move fast.

Looked in quickly at the office on the way home, but no reply to my memo from Hardacre so decided to call it a day.

Tried Butch Harness during *Nine O'clock News* despite severe looks from Angela Rippon.

Everything seemed to attach where it was meant to, and the all-important ring was a nice snug fit.

Instructions do not specify whether or not underpants to be worn. I understand there are men in responsible positions who are in the habit of going to the office pantless. I have often suspected Neville Pratt of being such a type, although I have no actual proof one way or another. Slipped into pants and trousers, therefore, and went into bathroom to check on effect, which as far as I could see was negligible. Have written myself a note in capital letters to BUY PAIR TIGHT JEANS a.s.a.p. tomorrow.

During weather forecast, noticed slight tingling sensation. Presume this to be 'physical pleasure' referred to on packaging. Must definitely wear it to work tomorrow and test it under field conditions.

A busy and interesting day all round. Am only sorry not to have heard yet about expenses. All this is costing me a lot of money.

Tuesday

Woke at 5.30 with a shock to realize I had completely forgotten to ring the Pedalows, Jane, etc., to explain about my presence in sex shop yesterday. Could not get back to sleep for worrying about it. Finally could stand suspense no longer and rang Tim shortly after 7.30. Vanessa answered. She did not sound pleased. Explained the situation as best I could and said I was sure she'd understand.

She said, 'Do you mean to tell me you woke us up at this ungodly hour to tell us you went to a sex shop yesterday?'

'It's not the *fact* that I went that matters,' I said, 'but the *reason* I'm anxious to get across.'

She said, 'You're a grown man now, Simon.' And she put the phone down.

There are some people with whom one can never say a thing without it being taken the wrong way.

Never mind. Better safe than sorry.

Had no sooner put the phone down than remembered I should have asked her for Jane's number.

To work wearing Harness. No one on underground appeared to notice or care. Am not sure whether I'm disappointed or relieved. Paused to examine trousers in shop windows and, to my eye, effect quite striking. It may have rated a niggardly five out of ten for 'visual pleasure', but for 'physical pleasure' it earned itself a considerably higher score. Alarmed to note, however, that by the time I reached office, weasel had gone curiously numb.

To loo at once to check on form. Horrified to discover it was quite blue and swollen.

Tried to remove Harness but ring completely stuck. Drastic steps clearly called for. Opened loo door and darted out into washroom to find soap. In my anxious state, forgot to pull up trousers and fell heavily on tiled floor knocking breath from my body just as Hardacre walked in.

'Hallo,' he said. 'On to deviationism already are we?' and walked out again before I could utter a word.

Crawled back into loo and closed door just as someone else came in. Realized I had forgotten to dampen soap, so had to do so with flushing loo water which sprayed up my arm, soaking my cuffs and half my sleeve.

Soaped weasel as best I could and by dint of much physical effort, not to say pain, succeeded after several minutes in easing ring off. Pain redoubled as circulation returned. So much so that compelled to sit there for fully fifteen minutes, despite furious bangings on door by desperate customer.

Thought about taking myself up to third floor to see Sister but decided too much explanation required. Finally plucked up strength to totter back to office to find Sue back at her desk doing her nails.

Her first words were, 'Why are you walking like Groucho Marx?'

'I've got a slight backache,' I replied.

Later, rang Fiona and fixed to have lunch with her at the Coconut Grove, wherever that may be.

Thought of ringing Theresa to get Jane's number, but obviously she has drawn her own conclusions about my meeting with Philippe anyway and did not wish to seem to be protesting too much. Gritted my teeth, therefore, and against my better judgement called Armitage instead.

He said, 'I thought you'd be sniffing around now Jane's no longer engaged.'

This was news to me but I was certainly not going to let him know that. I came back like a whiplash. 'Why must you assume that everyone's motives are base?' I said.

'Because,' he said, 'they usually are.'

I said wearily, 'If you don't know where Jane is, you only have to say so. There's no need to make a Margaret Drabble novel out of it.'

He said, 'Careful. Remember who you're speaking to. I'm that chap who holds the key to all those naughty places you dare not go to alone.' And he rang off.

I had a feeling that once one started to delve into this subject, all sorts of creepy-crawlies would come out of the woodwork.

Later, dictated memo to Hardacre.

Memo

To: Keith Hardacre
From: Simon Crisp   6 February

Surprised not have heard anything from you yet re my expenses. Have already spent nearly £65 of my own money on this project and the figure could easily rise to £100 or more before I've finished. Can we therefore agree an expenses budget a.s.a.p.?

Re personal involvement in research: have decided to play this by ear, as suggested.

S.C.

Home early after a long and action-packed day.

After supper, watched a fascinating TV programme about life at Radley College, the famous boys' public school. I seem to remember there was talk at one time of my going there. Or was it Repton? As it turned out, either would have been acceptable.

By a curious coincidence, programme focused on sex life of three rather precocious senior boys. We saw them campaigning for the Gay Liberation Front in school's mock elections, being interviewed in one of the studies, and taking part in a house dance to which girls had been invited.

This was fascinating stuff for any public school boy of my generation because, of course, in my day the nearest one ever came to meeting a girl in term-time was in a house play when one or two of the younger boys were dressed up to play the female parts. Anyone caught with an actual girl was for the high jump.

The rules were relaxed marginally in my last two years when a Sixth Form dance was arranged with a nearby girls' boarding school – or against, as my friend Rex Dunwoody so wittily put it.

It just goes to show how things have changed in public schools that the three boys featured were able to claim that they could cycle out and see their girlfriends from a neighbouring school every day if they felt like it, and that they were allowed to bring their own girls to the house dance.

On the strength of this excellent programme, am

seriously considering including a section on sex in the public schools.

Shall resist natural temptation to carry out my research in one of the so-called top schools – Eton, Winchester and so on – and go instead for the old *alma mater*. Terms of reference are so important in this kind of work, and to be in a position to compare schoolboy mores over a twenty-year period could be very interesting indeed. It's the sort of thing the *Sunday Times* might easily fall upon with whoops of joy, and possibly large sums of money.

Will ring the school secretary first thing in the morning. Or should I go straight to Dickie Dunmow? As a house-master, I seem to remember his being more open-minded than most. Except, that is, when it came to Latin verse.

Wednesday

Still far from comfortable. As an experiment, the Harness has been a bit of a flop all round. A quantitative survey at grass roots level of weasel envy/admiration could have made a fascinating footnote to the sex shop section – but not at the expense of impotence or possibly even gangrene.

To the office in sombre mood to find a memo from Hardacre awaiting me on my desk.

Memo

To: Simon Crisp, Special Projects Manager
From: Keith Hardacre, Deputy Managing Director

6 February

Thank you for your memo. Of course you will be reimbursed for any small out-of-pocket expenses that may arise in the course of your enquiries, such as taxi fares etc. But surely it should be possible to interview informants at a time and place where refreshments are not an automatic feature of the proceedings? Apart from the unnecessary expense incurred, I have personally found it almost impossible to concentrate and make useful notes at the same time as tackling half a lobster or pondering a wine list.

As far as the purchase of magazines etc. goes, most erotic literature is available on the open shelves these days and I should have thought it perfectly feasible for you to acquire all the information you need from such publications without in fact having to go so far as to purchase them.

I hope this answers your questions.

KH

Not so much answered as avoided, I'd say. Am beginning to wonder if the powers that be are taking the Crisp Report as seriously as they should.

After lunch, wrote to Dickie Dunmow explaining what I am up to and asking if it might be possible to come down to the old place and interview one or two boys of different ages regarding their attitudes to girls, sex etc. I shall be most interested to see what he has to say.

Odd that I have so far received no response to my advertisement in *Time Out*. Still, I daresay these things take time to filter through.

Thursday

Was looking through my girlie magazines last night when I chanced upon an advertisement featuring a man in a tight and extremely revealing pair of trousers. The copy read: 'BUST 'ER WITH THE THRUSTER. We'll guarantee that your smooth talk and witty repartee will not be the only thing to hold her attention when you're dressed up in your eye-catching new thrusting undergarment. Thanks to its unique and easy-to-wear design, THE THRUSTER will raise your confidence, her high hopes, and much else besides! Your quietly arrogant, obviously raring-to-go appearance will ensure that she is already looking forward to the end of the evening before it has even begun. And only you will know why!'

This could be just the thing I am looking for as a safe, effective replacement for my Butch Harness.

Do not quite understand why one needs to be over eighteen to order it but have decided to plump anyway. £6.95 plus 50p for postage and handling is surely not going to break the bank as far as Barfords is concerned, and the evidence it will inevitably throw up will be invaluable.

One often hears it said that women are not interested primarily in a man's appearance. We shall see.

Friday

Cannot believe I have had no replies to my advertisement, even though I did try to cut corners by not going for the semi-display.

Shortly before lunch, went down to post room to check if there were any letters for John Ashford. Who should I find there but the spotty messenger who tried to make a monkey out of me the other day. As I came in, he grinned at his friends in a knowing way and one or two of them tried unsuccessfully to conceal a snigger behind their hands.

Treated them to one of my famous icy stares and asked if they happened to have any letters for Mr Ashford.

The spotty one said, 'No one of that name working here, chief.' Unfortunately, he said it in such a serious tone of voice that it was impossible to tick him off for his obvious cheek.

I said, 'I hope you're telling me the truth. I happen to be using the name pseudonymously for a very important reason.'

'Enough said, squire,' he said, winking and tapping the side of his nose.

For two pins would have boxed his ears. As it was, left the room without a word. Caught my hip painfully against the edge of the counter as I did so, but I don't think anyone noticed.

A miracle occurred this afternoon when, for only the second time since joining the company, Agnes, the West Indian tea lady, actually brought me a cup without my having to ask her.

I said jokingly, 'Well, this is a turn-up for the books, Agnes.'

To my amazement she actually smiled at me, a thing I have only ever seen her do to her fellow Trinidadians. 'Big sexy man like you, Mr Samson,' she said, 'get everything he want from big sexy ladies.' And rolling her eyes and waggling her enormous hips, she traipsed out noisily on her large, slippered feet.

It would be nice to think that at least one member of the staff here accords me the degree of respect to which I am entitled, even if it is only the tea lady.

Was slipping on overcoat prior to leaving for home when Neville Pratt's new assistant, Matthew Chinnery, stuck his head round the door and tossed a large manilla envelope onto my desk. 'These found their way to me by mistake,' he said. 'Someone suggested they might be something to do with you. I can't imagine why.' And with a nod he disappeared.

Opened the envelope and out slipped half a dozen letters, pinned together, all addressed to Box 248 and all beginning 'Dear Attractive, Sensitive Stallion. . .' Was so embarrased, I shoved the whole lot into my briefcase and hurried out to the lift.

On way out of front door, spotted Chinnery and a couple of his cronies chatting with Dawn, the receptionist. As I passed, they straightened up, all innocence, needless to say. Glanced back quickly to find them giggling together and holding their noses like a lot of school-children.

Someone round here is to feel the rough side of my tongue before very long.

Weasel slightly better. I *would* say functioning normally, but unfortunately am not in a position to make such a claim.

Saturday

Less than three weeks to go before the report is due to be delivered, yet I feel I have barely scratched the surface of the subject so far.

Am all right on sex films, sex shops and the like, but what about live sex shows? Prostitution? Massage parlours? Adultery? Orgies? Homosexuality? The more I think about it, the more I wonder where it will all end.

George Washington really hit the nail on the head when he said 'So much to do, so little time'. Or was it Mahatma Gandhi?

Frankly, cannot wait for Beddoes to arrive on

Wednesday. Never have I been in as much need of good, practical advice as I am at this moment.

In the meantime, must press on with work in hand. After breakfast settled down to my *Time Out* letters. Had hoped that my intriguing wording might have attracted rather more replies, but six is a start, I suppose. There are probably more to come.

Am not quite sure what I'd been expecting. Perhaps nothing quite as crude as COME TO OUR ORGY invitations, but certainly one or two suggestions of a pretty blatant nature. Was surprised, therefore, by the first one I picked out:

Dear Attractive, Sensitive Stallion,
You sound very much my type and I should like to meet you. I am thirty years old but look younger, so my friends assure me! I am slightly on the tall side for some people's tastes. I am five foot eight inches, but slim, with a fairly good figure and lightish hair. I do not smoke and am not what you might call a drinker, except for the occasional glass of wine with my dinner! Like you I have a wide range of quite unusual tastes. I very much enjoy eating out in nice but not too expensive restaurants, theatre, films, walking in the country, animals, music (pop but not too heavy!), conversation, meeting people etc.

I see you are adventurous. I enjoy adventure too. Last year I took my moped to Normandy and had a fascinating camping holiday.

I don't know quite what you mean by free-thinking. I do not have any romantic attachments, but then, of course, if I did I wouldn't be writing to you!

Unfortunately, I do not happen to have a spare photograph of myself and anyway I'm not very photogenic. Perhaps it would be best if we were to meet for a drink and a chat and see how we get on before we start exchanging personal mementoes.

I look forward to receiving a call from you soon.

Yours sincerely,
Julie Brown

Her address was a street I have never heard of, somewhere in SE24.

Of the rest, one was matter of fact to the point of rudeness:

'You can have my phone number but not my photograph. If you want to send me a snap of yourself, that's up to you. You could be my type, but obviously I can't tell without meeting you. The next move is yours. You are the tenth ad I've replied to, so you'd better remember your box number when you ring.

Yours
Fran Holland

She'll need to write to more than ten if she's going to stand the slightest chance of success. Could she be one of these dominant types one gathers are all the rage these days? Am tempted to get in touch with her out of sheer curiosity. Ditto with 'Alan' who has seen fit to send me his business card without explanation.

Am also intrigued by short, sharp note from foreign girl called Marie-Lise. She doesn't say what nationality but I suspect French:

Hallo, stallion,
Not sure what you want but have written anyway. I am only twenty but am sophisticated and have been around. I enjoy good restaurants, travel by air, staying in first-class hotels, clothes, dancing etc. You say you know the score, so you will understand what I mean. Ring mornings only. If I am not in, you can leave your name on the answering machine. I look forward to hearing from you, big boy.

Thought it might be useful to have the foreigner's angle on sex in Britain, so took a bow at a venture and rang her number.

Surprised that she seemed to have such difficulty remembering our recent correspondence. Put this down at first to her lack of familiarity with the language, particularly when she started talking about services. Convinced that I had become unwittingly caught up with religion in some shape or form, I said that unfortunately I was not as regular about that sort of thing as I would like, but that I'd be prepared to fit in with her plans up to a certain point.

She said that depended on what I had in mind and started quoting large sums of money at me. By now I was in a complete muddle and told her that there had obviously been some sort of mistake.

She said, 'Those are my rates, take it or leave it.'

I said, 'In the circumstances, I think I'll leave it.'

'That's fine by me,' she said, 'you're the customer.'

I can only think that she thought I had something to do with a shop.

Decided that, all in all, Miss Brown sounded my best bet. She is probably very typical of the sort of people who look for love through the columns of magazines.

She sounded rather charming on the phone and seemed quite surprised that I had called. When I asked her why, she said, 'It's just that I wasn't sure whether I'd made myself sound attractive enough.'

We have arranged to meet for a drink in the bar at the Piccadilly Hotel on Monday evening at six. Am quite looking forward to my little adventure.

Had seriously thought of trying out one of these Paul Raymond sex shows that I am always passing in Soho and always meaning to investigate – *Rip Off* at the Windmill Theatre 'The Erotic Experience of the Modern Era, now in its 5th Great Year'; or *The Festival of Erotica* at Raymond's Revuebar 'New Acts, New Girls, New Thrills, now in its 23rd Sensational Year'.

They both sound pretty hot stuff.

In the end, though, decided to shelve both of them and take myself off to an altogether more congenial and familiar stamping ground, the National Theatre, to see if I couldn't squeeze into *The Romans in Britain*. There's been such a hooha about it recently.

Frankly, it takes more than a bit of full frontal male nudity to keep me awake at night, and besides, as Harold Hobson rightly said in his letter to *The Times*, one cannot begin to discuss a play as controversial as this without having seen it first.

Rumour had it that, what with the Leader of the Greater London Council, Sir Horace Cutler, walking out during a performance, and Mrs Whitehouse threatening to take everyone to court without even seeing it, it was impossible to get a ticket for love or money.

In the event, arrived a few minutes before curtain-up, bought myself a stand-by ticket for £3.50 without the slightest difficulty and took my seat in the eighth row.

An altogether fascinating evening. Strong meat it certainly is. I had no idea such language was bandied about or such things shown on the London stage. But then, strong subjects call for strong language and the famous homosexual rape occupied only a few moments out of nearly three hours. The only thing that upset me was that the nude young Celts made me feel so dreadfully overweight.

During the interval was standing in the bar when I overheard a bearded man saying to a woman, 'I mean, all right, if we have to have homosexual rape we have to have it. But quite honestly, as far as I'm concerned, there's just too much of everything.'

Suddenly something about the woman caught my eye. Looked at her more closely and realized with a shock that it was Enid Trubshawe, the mother of my ex-fiancée, Amanda, and the wife of my ex-chairman, Derrick. Whoever the bearded man was, it certainly wasn't her husband. What was more, he was holding her by the hand, and the looks she was giving him expressed considerably more than passing interest in his critical views.

Would happily have slipped away unobserved, but was so intrigued to find out what was going on that I could not resist calling out her name. Noticed she quickly unhitched her arm, and although she carried the whole thing off with her usual charm and elegance, the word guilt was written all over both their faces.

'Do you know Gerald Campsey-Ash?' she said in a vague, slightly wobbly voice.

I said that I'd never heard of him but that it was certainly a name with a nice old-fashioned English ring to it.

The man said, 'I'm Campsey-Ash and I happen to be Welsh.'

Enid explained that I had been, until recently, one of Derrick's bright young hopefuls.

'Bright at work perhaps,' he said.

'Gerald and I are great theatre goers,' Enid said.

'Oh yes?' I said, pretending innocence.

'You know what Derrick's like about the theatre. Luckily Gerald's got his finger in a lot of showbiz pies, so he's always getting tickets and rushing me off to all the best things. Derrick couldn't approve more.'

A more blatant case of the lady protesting too much I've yet to encounter.

I said casually, 'What do you think of the play? Pretty strong stuff, eh?'

'Personally I think it's rather fun,' she said.

Naturally, asked about Amanda. Enid had just about time to tell me that she was engaged to someone in the army when the bell went and we had to resume our seats.

Second half rather less sensational – although have a feeling its effect lessened slightly by (a) the shocking news of A.'s engagement and (b) my catching E. in obvious flagrante.

Have a distinct feeling I may have got my adultery chapter!

Sunday

Woke in the small hours in a cold sweat with the realization that I have made no headway whatever with homosexuality.

Apart from the man who ran the Workers' Workshop in Covent Garden I once attended with Victoria, I do not believe I have met any gays, as we must now learn to refer to them. At least, not knowingly.

Feel I should start making inroads into this strange world about which one hears so much but has such little personal experience. A gay nightclub would be an obvious starting point, but that could lead to all sorts of complications and misunderstandings.

Though hardly a young Lord Alfred Douglas, I am not without my good points and there's no knowing what these sort of people go for. I understand that some of them can be quite rough. The fate suffered by the young Druid at the hands of the brutish Roman soldiers is still too fresh in my mind for comfort.

So far completely stumped as to how this most delicate of areas should be tackled, but tackled it must be.

Got down to the Sunday papers soon after Alistair Cooke's *Letter from America*. What a first-class broadcaster he is. I somehow cannot imagine him sitting in his Fifth Avenue apartment riffling through dirty magazines or slipping furtively in and out of blue movie houses, even under the pretence of a journalistic assignment. His familiar voice only serves to remind me of how far I still have to go in order to achieve the big breakthrough that everyone needs to achieve public recognition.

Settled down in more sombre mood than usual with the Sunday papers. By an extraordinary coincidence, came upon a fascinating article about an apiarist called Howard Johnson who has just started up a thing called the National Campaign for the Knowledge, Encouragement and Rights of Sexual Freedom, or NACKERS for short.

Although Mr Johnson is not prepared at this stage to 'name names', he claims to have already enlisted the support of 'several distinguished public figures in the arts and public life' and believes that the tide of opinion is turning against the nation's most famous watchdog to such a degree that, before long, thousands will be flocking to his cause.

His campaign war cry is Stamp Out Do-Gooders, and he calls upon every man and woman in the country who believes in individual freedom to SOD along with him.

Must get in touch with Mr Johnson at the earliest opportunity.

Had been planning to spend afternoon working on critical appreciation of girlie magazines. However, in my book, Sunday is a day that should be devoted to the spirit rather than the flesh. I realize that everything God made is beautiful in its own particular way, but given a choice between grass, blue skies and fluffy white clouds, and thrusting bosoms and splayed crutches, I know which inspire me to nobler thoughts.

Set off for Hyde Park after lunch.

Every time I stroll there under the chestnuts, among the dogs and nannies and kite fliers, I find my thoughts turning to poor, sad, misunderstood little J.M. Barrie who trod these same wooded paths eighty years ago, plotting adventures for Peter Pan. I feel sure that, if only I had a nice dog to keep me company, my imagination would also be aroused to comparable heights.

Was sitting on one of the benches watching some middle-aged men sailing their model yachts when I overheard two small children deep in conversation.

He: 'You're a lesbian.'

She: 'So what? You're a homosexual.'

He (after suitable pause for thought): 'Well, what about intercourse then?'

She: 'What about it?'

He: 'I don't know, but I don't think it's very nice.'

Home for tea and crumpets and the children's Sunday serial on BBC TV.

A charming and welcome interlude in this strange period of my life. They say that sex keeps you young, but I'm beginning to think quite the opposite is true.

Monday, 12 February

A dismal Monday morning, made more so by cold, damp drizzle and the phone call I received from Ruth Macmichael ringing from Harley Preston to ask what all this was she had heard about my spending my time among the strip clubs and peep shows of Soho.

Had forgotten how aggressive she can be on the phone when she wants and how quickly she can get one's hackles up with her abrasive trans-Atlantic manner.

I said politely, 'If you are referring to the report I am compiling on the state of British morals in the 1980s, I'm sure we can arrange to have a copy sent to you as soon as it is published.'

'Jesus,' she said, 'you're even more full of shit than I remember. You English guys are all the same. Your idea of the sexual revolution is buying *Penthouse* and not wrapping it inside the evening paper. You don't deserve to be allowed near women, you know that? Treat them rough and they'll respect you for it, right? The idea that a woman might have a mind of her own never even comes into it.'

Tried to put my point of view, but once these American women get the bit between their teeth there's no stopping them.

'Your whole approach is an insult to women,' she went on, 'and if your report comes out the way I think it will, then watch out, baby, because the shit's really going to start flying, and I mean flying. I'm only trying to help you because I kind of feel responsible for you – even though you are an ass-hole.'

I said, 'Thank you for your advice, although frankly I cannot see it is any of your business.'

'On the contrary,' she replied. 'As a woman who is sick to death of being exploited as a sex object, I think it is very much my business.'

The mistake all these women libbers make is in assuming that any man is the slightest bit interested in them from any point of view whatever. Indeed, if I was as unattractive to look at and listen to as the majority of them, I'd keep very quiet indeed.

I said politely, 'In that case, perhaps you would care to suggest in which areas one *should* be looking?'

'Try TV commercials, popular song lyrics and jokes for a start,' she said. 'They'll tell you far more about the way people are thinking about sex than any amount of blue movies.'

I said, 'Oh, I'm sorry; I thought you were going to tell me something I didn't know.' And before she could utter another word, I put the phone down on her. She may have a point or she may not. For the time being, I'd prefer to keep an open mind on the subject.

In the meantime, have many more urgent matters on my plate – adultery being not the least among them. Have shilly-shallied for long enough over this one, and the time has now come for action.

Rang The Boltons shortly before noon. Interested to find that Enid's voice still affects me as strongly as ever. I merely said that I wished to see her on a matter of some delicacy.

She said, 'You always were a mysterious young man.' I did not deny it.

I am to lunch with her at The Boltons on Thursday.

To the Piccadilly Hotel after work for my blind date with Miss Brown. Chose a corner table with a good view of the entrance, ordered a large whisky and soda, sat back and took in the scene.

Few things appeal more to the imaginative temperament than the transient life of a big city hotel. Oscar Wilde, Arnold Bennett, Kipling, Hemingway – these are just a few of the artists who have produced some of their best work in hotels and one can see why. After only a few minutes in the Piccadilly bar, my fingers began to itch for the typewriter keys and ideas for no less than three short stories sprang unbidden to my mind.

After a few minutes, a stunning blonde with a magnificent figure dressed in black walked into the bar, looked around briefly and sat at the next table but one to me. She was obviously waiting for somebody. At one point, caught her eye and smiled knowingly but I don't think she can have seen me.

Finished my drink to discover it was already twenty past six. Strolled out to lobby on off-chance there had been a misunderstanding re exact location of rendezvous. No one obviously looking for anyone, so returned to bar and ordered another drink.

Blonde girl also showing signs of having been stood up. At 6.30 nipped to loo and came back to find her talking animatedly to a swarthy, rather Arabic-looking chap with a moustache. There are those who find middle-eastern looks attractive but I can't see it myself and I must admit to feeling rather disappointed by the girl's taste. She was probably one of those loose creatures one hears about who hang around in hotel lobbies in the West End, touting for business with oil sheiks.

Finally decided enough was enough. Paid my bill and was about to leave when my date appeared from the direction of the lobby and stood in the entrance to the bar, looking about her in an obvious way.

As I'd suspected, Miss Brown had overstated her charms. I suppose I couldn't blame her, but still, I hadn't imagined she would turn out to be *quite* so plump, nor that she would be the type to wear quite so much make-up. Put it down to nervousness. That or an unfortunate complexion.

On the other hand, it was only work as far as I was concerned. I wasn't being asked to marry the girl. Took a deep breath and strolled across to her. 'Hallo,' I said. 'I'm Simon Crisp.'

'I wouldn't give a monkey's if you was the Aga Khan, darling,' she said. 'I'm booked this evening.' And she walked back into the lobby, followed shortly afterwards by the blonde and her Arabic boyfriend.

Hung around for a few more minutes, but at seven o'clock decided to call it a day. Ate a disgusting hamburger at one of these plastic American-style places and felt slightly sick.

Arrived home to find that my suit stank to high heaven of fried food. Also that I had stepped in a dog dirt somewhere and walked it all over the flat.

Would have changed and gone out to the local Odeon for the last performance of *The Blue Lagoon*, but assumed Miss Brown would be ringing with an explanation. Wrongly, as it turned out.

To bed at midnight with a mug of Milo and the new Ed McBain. Milk slightly sour and lumpy.

Like Ruth Macmichael.

Tuesday

A beautiful sunny day. Along with the clouds have disappeared all my worries and irritations of yesterday, and a clear blue sky heralded one of the great events of my life and one which will certainly set Beddoes by the ears and no mistake: lunch with Fiona Richmond.

Bathed and shaved with special care – rather too special unfortunately since the new blade nicked my neck in no fewer than four places. Also washed hair. Breakfasted lightly and cleaned teeth well afterwards. Am not a great believer in the philosophy of the after-shave lotion; however, more by way of a controlled experiment than for reasons of personal advancement, I decided to try some out on Fiona.

Chose one that I was given for Christmas two years ago and which I understand to be particularly favoured by women. Slapped it on enthusiastically only to remember too late about the nicks on my neck. Quickly tried to wash it off with a soaking flannel but even so the pain was excruciating. Also got water down my shirt front.

Was halfway to work when I realized I had chosen a shirt with a particularly tight collar, so that every time I turned my head it gave my nicks a nasty little tug. By the time I arrived at the office, my neck a mass of small red spots and my collar flecked with blood.

Could not decide whether to buy something that would conceal ravaged neck or splurge out two or three quid on a new shirt.

Arrived in office just as phone was ringing. It was Miss Brown. In the circumstances, adopted a considerably sharper tone than is my wont.

I said, 'I rather thought you might have phoned last night.'

'*Me?*' she exclaimed. 'Phone *you*?'

'Well,' I said, 'you did stand me up.'

She said, 'I like that! I sat there for half an hour and there was no sign of you.'

I said, 'Sat where? Euston Station?'

'What's Euston Station got to do with it?' she said. 'We agreed to meet in the bar of the Piccadilly Hotel and that's where I was. Why? Were you at Euston?'

'No, of course not,' I said. 'I was at the Piccadilly too.'

She said, 'Well, why didn't you come and talk to me? I gave you a perfectly good description.'

I said, 'All right. Let me tell you. I sat there for an *hour* and the only single girl I saw in all that time was a very glamorous blonde who told the waiter she was waiting for someone.'

'Of course, you idiot,' she said. 'You.'

I said, 'Do you mean to tell me that that was you?'

'How many other single women did you count?' she said.

I said, 'But you went off with some ghastly middle-eastern type.'

She said, 'If you must know, he's my cousin and he's neither ghastly nor is he from the middle east. He happens to live in Romford and our meeting was entirely fortuitous. Since you obviously decided to rat on our arrangement, he took me out to dinner.'

I said, 'But this is a ghastly misunderstanding. I mean, what's a girl like you doing answering advertisements in Lonely Hearts columns?'

She said, 'I've no idea. But if you're the sort of person one ends up with, I don't think I'll bother again.'

Consoled myself with thought of lunch with Fiona.

Slipped out after coffee and bought myself a small tin of make-up. Chose as neutral a colour as I could find.

The young girl who served me said, 'I think you'll find it'll suit your colouring very well. My boyfriend swears by it, and he's slightly dark too.' No comment.

Just time to dash off a quick memo to Hardacre.

Memo

To: Keith Hardacre
From: Simon Crisp   13 February

Re: *Your memo of the 6th*

As you know, I'm the last to mix pleasure with business.
On the other hand, I feel it would be a pity to spoil the ship
for ha'p'orth of tar. Wouldn't you agree?

S.c.

Unfortunately, with Sue being off with a cold and my
typing being rather on the rusty side, plus an unusual
shortage of taxis, had to apply make-up to neck en route
and arrived at Coconut Grove rather later than I'd hoped
and in a muck sweat.

Luckily, Fiona delayed too, so was able to be at table to
greet her when she arrived. Was mildly disappointed that
when the waiter showed her across, more heads did not
turn and stare. But perhaps the sort of people who frequent
places like this are used to celebrities.

Happily, one of the waiters must have recognized her
because, before we had time to order one of their exotic
cocktails, someone came across and offered us each a glass
of champagne on the house.

Am often reading interviews with TV and film stars in
which the writer sets the scene by telling us that he met his
subject in this restaurant or that bar, and embellishes the
questions and answers with descriptions of who ordered
what, and how they sipped at their white wine and Perrier
water as they talked.

Hardacre is right for once. One obviously has to be very
experienced at journalism of this type to be able to order,
eat, drink and take in the atmosphere of the place at the
same time as asking all the right questions and writing
down the answers. For while I came away with a definite
impression of having enjoyed an excellent couple of hours
in the company of a friendly and amusing girl, I can recall
very little of our conversation.

I suppose I *was* rather nervous and perhaps four glasses of wine *is* excessive for someone who never normally drinks at lunchtime, but surely not so excessive as all that?

Nor are my notes very much help. Have read them through several times and am no nearer deciphering the illiterate scrawl than before. They read: 'Big with school-boys – more humour – Mayfair definitive old men – pussy sculpted – larger than life – blue and silver – looks like a shoe – Penthouse frilly aprons? – 16-year-old virgin up to 70-year-old something – like to move it while doing it – estate agent – ring up Arabian embassy – heavy with orgies – pillow sniffing – very geometrical.'

What can it all mean?

I do remember one curious incident. As we were getting up to leave, she said, 'Are you in any way connected with the theatre?'

I told her that I had always been a keen theatregoer and, where possible, first-nighter, and that I had been very much involved in amateur theatricals at Oxford.

She said, 'Yes, I know. You told me all that the other night. What I meant was, are you by any chance perform-ing now? I mean today?'

Remembering her famous 'road-testing' series, was suddenly struck by the thought that by 'performing' she might be referring to something quite different. However, did not wish to appear to be taking too much for granted, so waited until we got out into the street, slipped a hand under her elbow and said quietly, 'Of course, there are performances and performances.'

'You're telling me,' she said.

I gave a light knowing laugh and hailed a cab. 'Where to?' I asked her as she climbed in.

'Bayswater,' she said, closed the door and drove away, leaving me standing on the pavement.

Gave my chin a puzzled rub and found my hand covered in some strange sticky brown substance.

As soon as I got back to office, went straight to gents to discover that the make-up I had applied to my neck had run down into my collar and mingled with the bloodstains to create as unattractive an effect as I have seen since that day at school when Kippax's boil burst.

Only hope this had nothing to do with Fiona's abrupt

decision to break off our cordial dialogue. If so, it was a cruel stroke of fate. I suppose I can't blame her. You certainly wouldn't catch me testing a man who appeared to be in the latter stages of bubonic plague.

Still, the more I think about it, the more I am sure I am well out of it. Fiona has a wicked sense of humour and I should hate to find myself portrayed as one of her rare failures. Was thinking of ringing her to explain about neck, but frankly, if ever there was a case of quitting while one is ahead, it is this.

Shouldn't wonder if I don't see a sudden change of attitude from the messenger boys. F. is very popular among teenagers and it's only a matter of time before news of my relationship with her filters through to the post room. If I have anything to do with it, that is.

Wednesday

The most bizarre start to a day that I can remember for many a year. Was in bath when front door bell went. I called out, 'Leave it on the mat and I'll collect it in a minute.'

A girl's voice replied, 'I can't. This has to be delivered in person.'

Scrambled out of bath, threw a towel round my waist and flung open door to be confronted by a couple of extremely buxom girls dressed in skimpy gym tunics and school boaters, with their hair done up in pigtails. Before I could open my mouth, they began to sing at me at the tops of their voices.

The next thing I knew, Miss Weedon from the flat opposite had opened her door and was standing there in her dressing gown and curlers, with Poppy her nasty little pug barking under her arm. At that moment, realized that the girls were in fact delivering a sung message of an extremely suggestive nature, finishing up with words to the effect that they hoped today would be a memorable Valentine's Day that I would remember for years to come.

I do not think I have ever been more embarrassed in my life.

Had I been fully dressed, I daresay I could have carried off the situation with a witty riposte that would have sent all of us, including Miss Weedon, off to work with a smile on our faces and, who knows, perhaps even a song in our hearts.

Unfortunately, am never at my wittiest when half naked and soaking wet, especially at eight o'clock in the morning. Looking the girls firmly in the eye I said, 'I'm sorry, there must be some mistake,' and closed the door firmly and politely in their faces.

As I walked back to the bathroom, one of them called through the letter box, 'There's more to come. Don't you want the rest of it?'

I called back over my shoulder, 'One verse is more than enough for me,' and got back into my bath.

A certain amount of whispering and giggling ensued, followed by high-pitched barking, some screams and Miss Weedon's voice calling out, 'And don't come back. This is a respectable block of flats. Not a music hall.'

My reputation amongst members of the residents' association is shaky enough as it is without my having it further damaged by accusations of gross moral turpitude.

An even greater worry is the realization that, for the first time in fifteen years, I have forgotten to send Mother a Valentine card. I don't seem to be able to get anything right these days.

To Roland Gardens en route for the office to interview the founder of NACKERS. A short tubby man in a tight-fitting black and yellow striped jersey opened the door to me and introduced himself as Howard Johnson. He took me through to a sitting room filled with cases of stuffed bees, offered me a cup of tea and disappeared into the next room. He appeared a few minutes later bearing two small wooden bowls filled with some steaming and curiously smelling liquid. Whatever it was, it certainly wasn't PG Tips.

'It's a little honey and herbal mixture of my own devising,' he explained. 'A real pick-me-up at this time of the morning, I always find.'

For him perhaps, but not for me. Pretended to sip at it before placing it on floor beside me.

We had a most fascinating talk about the rights and wrongs of censorship. I can quite see how some people might find Howard and his ideas rather extreme, and I am not entirely persuaded that anything should go on stage, screen and on TV. Like Mother, I am not exactly looking forward to the day when we shall be treated to the sight of people doing big potties in our sitting rooms.

On the other hand, Howard is quite right. People should be shocked from time to time. I was shocked by parts of *The Romans in Britain* and I certainly feel a better man for it.

Nor apparently am I alone in my radical thinking. John Mortimer, Clement Freud, Melvyn Bragg, Moira Lister, Janet Suzman, Ted Willis, Derek Nimmo – these are just a few of the public figures Howard is thinking of approaching with a view to their becoming NACKERS committee members. Not only that, but he has asked me if I would also be prepared to serve. Have not committed myself entirely yet, but have said I will give the matter serious thought. I have long been aware that, when it comes to standing up and being counted, I have been sadly backward in coming forward. This could be just the opportunity I have been looking for to break into public life in no uncertain terms.

Have in the meantime agreed to act as steward at a NACKERS public meeting to be held in the Smith-Beresford Rooms in Bloomsbury on Sunday week. Hope there won't be any trouble. One court appearance a year is more than enough for a man in my position.

Left for Heathrow in good time to meet Beddoes' plane. Even so, became caught up in traffic jam at Talgarth Road roundabout and another at airport underpass, and only just arrived in time.

Rushed inside to find plane delayed by twenty minutes. Unable to park, so drove round for a while listening to radio. Needle of petrol gauge obviously faulty because suddenly ran out and had to push car to petrol pumps. As a results, arrived back at terminal several minutes later than expected.

Passengers pouring out of customs but no sign of Beddoes.

After a while, stream became a thin trickle and finally dried up altogether. Asked member of airline staff if Brussels passengers through yet.

He said, 'Good Lord yes. They've all been and gone half an hour ago.'

I said, 'But the notice board said the plane was twenty minutes late.'

'Obviously it changed its mind,' he said.

Waited another half an hour, but still no sign of him. Drove back to Holland Park in a rage. Sat about in the flat twiddling my thumbs and doing desultory dusting until half past eight.

By now feeling decidedly hungry. Remembered I had not bought any food because expecting to eat out with Beddoes. Rushed round corner to delicatessen to find the manager locking the door and walking off up the street.

Arrived back in flat as phone was ringing. Picked it up to hear Beddoes' cheery voice saying that he was at Victoria Station and why hadn't I been at the airport to meet him?

I told him that I certainly had been there and, more to the point, where had he been?

He said, 'I hung about in the central concourse, then went to have a drink in the Panorama Bar.'

I said, 'There's no Panorama Bar at Heathrow.'

He said, 'Who said anything about Heathrow? I was at Gatwick.'

Sat through an indifferent western followed by Barry Norman making facetious comments about films which I had neither seen nor, in most cases, wished to.

Beddoes finally turned up at 11.30, rather the worse for drink, I thought. 'Cheers,' he kept saying as he wandered round the room, sitting on each of the chairs in turn and messing up the carefully plumped cushions.

I said, 'All I can say is thank heavens you arrived before I put my pyjamas on. I'm starved. Where are we eating?'

'I've no idea where you're going,' he said. 'I've eaten already and frankly I'm ready for my bed. Nightcap first though.' And he reached into a plastic bag and produced a half-empty quart bottle of Famous Grouse whisky. 'Nothing like it for staving off the old pangs,' he said. 'Puts hairs on your chest too. You could do with a few.'

I remember being told once by a nutritionist that one should never make the mistake of substituting alcohol for good nourishing food. She obviously does not suffer from thoughtless and unreliable friends. By one o'clock we'd finished the Grouse and heard all about Beddoes' latest amorous exploits in Amsterdam, when he gave a loud belch and said, 'Well, it's the steaming pit for me, laddie. Got to get myself in shape for the next few days.'

Reminded him of our night life arrangement.

'I am,' he said yawning loudly, 'entirely at your disposal. You tell me what you want and I'll lay it on – within reason of course. Oh, by the way, I'd almost forgotten. What happened to those two lovely schoolgirls? I thought you might have asked them back this evening.'

I might have guessed Beddoes had a hand in it somewhere.

I said, 'Oh them. Was that your idea? Rather amusing, I thought. Where did you find them?'

He tapped the side of his nose. 'Oh, you know, laddie,' he said. 'Friends of friends, if you get my meaning. I trust they provided the full service. At those prices they should have given you a haircut and redecorated the sitting room.'

'Actually', I said, 'I thought one verse made the point more than adequately.'

Beddoes frowned. 'But they did come in and . . . er . . . everything, didn't they?'

'Certainly not,' I said. 'I was in the bath at the time and very late for work. I merely thanked them and sent them packing.'

Beddoes seemed appalled. He said, 'But they had strict instructions to give you a Valentine's Day greeting that you would remember till the day you die.'

Beddoes has an irritating tendency to talk in riddles when he's had a few drinks, and frankly I was in no mood to pursue the matter further.

I said, 'Well, whatever it was they were meant to do, the point was well made and much appreciated. Thank you for going to all that expense on my behalf.'

'You must be joking if you think I can afford that sort of thing on the salaries they pay us in Brussels,' he said. 'No, I told them to charge it to you at Barfords. I knew you'd have a decent expense account.'

Thursday

Finally collapsed into bed shortly before two, only to be woken a few minutes later by an insistent ringing on the front door bell. Answered it to find myself face to face with a scraggy blonde with a marked Scottish accent, dressed from head to toe in red tartan, asking if Ralph was at home.

I replied, not very graciously I'm afraid, that it was true that he was a guest in my home and who should I say was asking for him?

She said that her name was Norma, that she was an air hostess, that she had met Beddoes on the flight over that evening, and that, on learning that she had problems over accommodation, he had given her my address and said that I'd be only too happy to offer her a bed.

At that moment, Beddoes appeared in the doorway of his room, dressed, as usual, in nothing but his towelling dressing gown. 'Oh good,' he said to Norma, putting an arm round her waist. 'I thought you might have lost the address.'

'No such luck,' she said, and smiled in a knowing sort of way.

Beddoes called out to me, 'Don't bother to stay up, laddie. I can manage on my own now.'

Turned into my own room, but could not resist a final crack. 'Don't mind me,' I said. 'Help yourself. I only live here.'

'Thanks,' said Beddoes, 'I already have.' And he held up a bottle of whisky I'd carefully concealed in the larder in case of emergency. With that the two of them disappeared into the bedroom.

I had forgotten how noisy Beddoes and his women can be when Sportsnighting is under way. Evidently Brussels has done nothing to dampen his ardour. *Au contraire*. I simply cannot imagine what he can possibly get up to that induces such a bedlam.

Am beginning to suspect he's the sort of man who uses a weasel enlarger. Also seriously considering introducing him to Ruth Macmichael. She'd take him down a peg or two and no mistake.

Morning post uninspiring except for a letter from Dickie Dunmow saying he couldn't quite understand what I was after but suggesting I come down to the school on Monday week and we can talk it over. Is it worth my while mugging up some Catullus between now and then, I ask myself? It might make all the difference.

On the way out to work called out to Beddoes and

reminded him we had some important business to complete.

'Haven't we all, laddie?' he called out.

Beddoes is like the flu. When you haven't got it, you can't for the life of you remember what all the fuss was about, and the moment you do, all you can think about is how soon it will go away again.

Arrived at office shortly after 9.30 to find Sue already at her desk, telephone at her ear and pencil poised over pad. Could not believe my eyes. When she'd finished I said, 'Well, this is a turn-up for the books. What are you up to? A little research of your own?'

'Actually,' she said, 'I was making an appointment at the hairdresser. Must fly.'

Onee again compelled to open my own mail.

She arrived back just as I was leaving for lunch with Enid. I hardly recognized her. All the straggly rat-tails had completely disappeared, to be replaced by a neat gamin cut which makes her look about fifteen. I had never realized before what a pretty girl she can be when she tries. She has the most enormous eyes, a perfect complexion and excellent bone structure. Must admit was completely bowled over.

In matters of sex I have always maintained that one must let the heart rule the head. Women invariably respond to a man who catches them unawares and bowls them over, and when, on a mad impulse, I asked her to join me for a drink after work, I can't say I was all that surprised that she accepted.

Set off for The Boltons feeling more confident than I can remember for years. Enid as charming and poised as ever in navy blue. My exuberant high spirits obviously infectious. I have never seen her on better form.

We had a delicious hot prawn dish to start with, followed by saddle of lamb and syllabub, with a Niersteiner, a Château Talbot and brandy.

Although far from tight, I was certainly merry and told some excellent jokes of a slightly risqué nature which she was obviously too ladylike to laugh at out loud, but clearly relished in her own quiet way.

Though not normally a great tittle-tattler, could not resist giving her the lowdown on the famous Harold Hill affair. After all, it's not every day that chairmen of large companies like Barfords elope with one's secretary.

'Are you quite sure you should be telling me all this?' she asked.

'Oh why not?' I said. 'We're people of the world, and you're not going to tell me your husband hasn't been tempted to stray from the straight and narrow before now.'

Was congratulating myself on my deftness at drawing the conversation round to the question of adultery in general and hers in particular, and was surprised that she should appear so puzzled by my comment.

She said, 'I'm afraid I'm not quite with you.'

I winked and said, 'Well, you know . . . power being the most potent aphrodisiac and so on.'

Enid put down her glass. 'Are you saying that Derrick is unfaithful to me?' she asked.

It has always been a golden rule with me that once one has got into a thing one must have the courage of one's convictions and carry it through to the end with style and panache.

'All I'm saying,' I said, 'is that in an open marriage like yours – and I'm not saying anything against open marriages . . .'

She said, 'This is all gibberish to me. What's an open marriage in normal, everyday speech?'

I said, 'Sorry about the sociological jargon. What I mean is, you go your way, so I am presuming he goes his.'

'I don't know where you got this idea from,' she said. 'As far as I am aware, we are both going in approximately the same direction.'

Sorely tempted to get out notebook and jot down *aide memoire* re behaviour of people when caught out in adulterous situations, but did not wish to inhibit her in any way.

'Approximately,' I prompted. 'Except of course for theatre-going.'

'What is all this about?' she asked, suddenly rather cross.

Decided it was time to bring things to a head. 'Enid,' I said. 'I'm talking about adultery and you know it. I'm talking about the National Theatre and *The Romans in*

Britain and you and Gerald whatever-his-name-is.'

She burst into shrieks of laughter. 'Me?' she said. 'And Gerald? Are you mad? He's my brother.'

This may or may not have been a clever cover-up. At all events, decided not to pursue the matter further at this stage. Nor to ask after Amanda.

Back to the office in pensive mood to find a message from Beddoes asking me to ring him as soon as possible.

Rang the flat and got engaged signal. Knowing Beddoes of old, assumed he was still occupied with Norma and had taken phone off hook in order not to be disturbed, so thought no more about it. Repeated the process at approximately ten-minute intervals for the next hour with similar results. By now beginning to experience familiar signs of irritation with which Beddoes is so closely identified in my mind.

Finally, in a rage, rang exchange to explain that I was the Middlesex Hospital trying to contact a brain surgeon who had absent-mindedly left his phone off the hook and would they mind putting the screamer on, since this was something of an emergency.

The girl said she would just try the number herself and came back in a moment or two later with the news that 'the subscriber was in conversation'.

I said, 'In point of fact, *I* happen to be the subscriber. He is merely a guest in my house. Executives at the European Commission may not be familiar with telephone bills but we are.'

The girl said, 'I thought you said your friend's a brain surgeon.'

'He helps out part-time,' I said. 'Still, if you're not prepared to put yourself out to save lives, that's your decision.'

Finally got through. Beddoes as cool as a cucumber in the face of my fury. He said, 'What do you think I've been doing on the phone for the last couple of hours?'

I said, 'Ringing friends apparently.'

'Quite,' he said. 'Not perhaps friends in the sense that you'd understand the word, but they're certainly always very friendly to me whenever I ring up.'

'You don't mean prostitutes, do you?' I said.

'If you must put it so crudely,' he said, 'yes.'

I said, 'You did point out, I hope, that I only want to interview them? I think we can take the hanky-panky for granted.'

'*You* may be able to,' he said.

I decided the time had come to get a few things straight. I said, 'Now look here, Beddoes. I'm very grateful to you for your help in this matter, but I'm afraid I have a limited budget, and if you think I am going to be a party to your having a good time at Barfords' expense, I'm afraid you've got another think coming.'

Beddoes chuckled. 'We'll see, laddie,' he said. 'We'll see.'

We certainly shall.

Got into the lift at one point in the afternoon to find myself face to face with the spotty messenger and a couple of his cronies. Tried to pretend they weren't there, but their ill-disguised sniggers and obscene gestures final provoked me to speech.

I said, 'Were you a better behaved bunch, I'd have brought my friend, Fiona Richmond, down to the post room to meet you all.'

'Oh what a shame,' said Spotty, 'because I was going to introduce you to Raquel Welch.'

To the Horse's Neck Wine Bar for a drink with Sue at 5.30. For someone of only nineteen she really does have an excellent sense of humour. Could not resist a little gentle probing re her friendship with Bryant-Fenn.

'Who?' she said.

'Hugh,' I said. 'Hugh Bryant-Fenn. You know. Old Sex Pistol. Blue films in Ashford and all that.'

'Oh,' she said vaguely, 'I'd forgotten all about him. Isn't he a friend of yours or something?'

'Sort of,' I said. 'And yours, too, I thought.'

'Hardly,' she said. 'Poor old chap. He needs a psychiatrist, not a girlfriend. They're all the same, these middle-aged swingers. All talk and no action.'

I said, still feigning innocence, 'But I'd always understood him to be something of a ladies' man. He has a considerable reputation.'

'If he has,' she said, 'it's entirely in his own mind.' And to my delight she went on to describe how she, too, had fallen prey to his famous red book ploy.

She said, 'I can't see the point of all that slow build-up stuff myself. It nearly always means there's nothing at the end of it. I mean, if a bloke takes you back to his place for the obvious reason, either he wants to get on with it or he doesn't.'

It is not often a girl sets my heart racing these days, but talking to Sue, I could feel the years dropping away from me. It was as if I were twenty-one again.

I said, 'I couldn't agree more. I'm a man of action and few words myself, as you've probably realized. I think girls can pretty well reckon to know where they stand with me.'

Asked her if she was doing anything for dinner tomorrow night. She said that, by an odd coincidence, she and her flatmates were throwing a small party and why didn't I come? Evidently she doesn't think of *me* as being middle-aged, and who can blame her?

I said that unfortunately I had a friend staying.

She said, 'Bring him too. We could do with some more men.'

Is it my imagination or did she place a little extra emphasis on the word 'men'?

Beddoes out again when I got home. He arrived back with Norma at about 10.30, made coffee, poured out the last remaining drops of my whisky and settled in front of the TV set.

I said, 'Actually I was rather hoping to have a look at the theatre awards. I've seen them every year now for seven years.'

Later, as he was on his way to bed with Norma, I asked him if by any chance he knew how one went about finding an orgy.

I might have been asking him to introduce me to the head of the Mafia from the look of pained disbelief that crossed his face. 'What do you take me for?' he said. 'A sex maniac?'

I don't know why I bother.

Friday

Time is running out and I am still no nearer finding an orgy. Am still convinced the chairman's secretary, Erica, knows more than she cares to admit, and decided the moment had come to put my theory to the test. To my surprise, got straight through to chairman who informed me rather sharply that Miss Thompson was out shopping. For what? one wondered. Kinky gear perhaps?

In order not to waste time, slipped out to see if I could track down any of these contact magazines in which, if Pratt is to be believed, people advertise their peculiar interests.

Had understood that publications of this nature freely available on newsagents' stands etc. Consequently had embarrassing conversation with newspaper seller near Piccadilly Circus underground station who got it into his head that I was a keen amateur electrician and kept trying to palm me off with magazines dealing with computers and electronics. In the end I'm afraid one or two heated words were exchanged. It was all quite unnecessary.

Eventually tried 'adult' magazine shop. Place strangely deserted except for one young man with Scottish accent standing at cash desk discussing the gay scene in London with shop manager.

Shelves well-stocked with the sort of publications I had in mind. Tried to look inside to make sure but all stuck together with sellotape. Picked out two anyway – *In Touch* and *Hallo*. £3.50 each.

Had just settled down with *Hallo* and sardine and tomato sandwich in office when Beddoes rang to say that his lunch date in the City had fallen through and would I care to stand in for his guest?

You don't live with somebody as long as I have lived with Beddoes to know something about their tastes in food, and his are lower than average. Have never myself subscribed to this craze for so-called fast-food, which the Americans will insist on forcing down our throats, and sitting about in some garishly lit plastic and formica establishment chewing soggy chips and tasteless rissoles out of a cardboard box is not my idea of a gastronomic treat. Thanked him therefore for the kind thought and told him that, with so much on hand, was having a working lunch.

'What a pity,' he said. 'You're always saying how much you'd like to eat at the Connaught. Never mind. Another time. See you later anyway. Shall we say six o'clock in the bar of the Mayfair?'

To coffee machine, only to discover something had gone wrong again with the selector mechanism, so that I ended up with a cup of hot water.

Have always been told that many more people advertise their charms and special interests than one might think, but had never realized it was done quite as blatantly as it is in this sort of publication. If the black and white snaps which accompany many of the ads are anything to go by, I can hardly believe that many of them produce a single reply. My age-old theory about sexiness being nearest to ugliness has never looked closer to holding water.

Might seriously consider following up one or two of the more colourful suggestions on offer if only one knew what one was letting oneself in for. It's the sort of world where, if you don't know what you're up to, it could all too easily end in tears.

By the same token, was not exactly over the moon at the prospect of the evening's entertainment. Whatever it was that Beddoes had laid on, I could only hope it would not involve dressing up in a PVC mac and having my bottom smacked.

A propos of which, suddenly realized to my horror that I had become so caught up in my research that I had completely forgotten to cash a cheque. Bank now closed, ditto cashiers. Would girls take American Express? The phrase 'That'll do nicely, sir' suddenly acquired a whole new meaning.

After quick wash and brush-up, set off shortly before six for the Mayfair.

Beddoes tried very hard to appear nonchalant, but any fool could see he was as excited as a schoolboy on his first outing to London.

I said, 'What were you thinking of doing about dinner?'

'Hadn't thought,' said Beddoes, swigging his vodka and tonic. 'I'm easy. A hamburger will do me fine. I couldn't face another heavy meal after the Connaught.'

'Who did you ask in the end?' I said.

'No one,' he said. 'I just ate for two.'

In the end, after more drinks and a bowl or two of peanuts, had completely lost appetite. At least Beddoes had the grace to offer to pay. Not that that did a lot towards alleviating the feeling of faint nausea that swept over me as we rumbled past Harrods. Matters not helped by Beddoes' particularly evil-smelling cheroot. I'm surprised the taxi driver didn't say something.

I remarked that we appeared to be heading away from the part of London traditionally associated in one's mind with ladies of the night. Beddoes merely laughed and said, 'Wait and see, laddie.'

Eventually we drew up outside a terraced house in a street off Redcliffe Square, of all the unlikely venues. While I paid off the taxi, Beddoes announced our arrival over the entryphone.

The taxi driver said to me under his breath, 'Ought to be ashamed of yourselves.'

When I asked him what he meant, he said, 'Don't blame me if your whatsit drops off,' and drove away up the street.

Was sorry not to be going with him.

We made our way up the broad, carpeted staircase to the third floor and paused for breath outside No. 5.

The door was opened by a comfortable-looking middle-aged woman in a blue patterned, frock. Her greying hair was done up in a rather elaborate style and a pair of spectacles hung by a cord round her neck.

'Mr Cripps?' she asked in a quiet, educated voice.

'Six out of ten,' said Beddoes. 'I'm Beddoes, he's Crisp. By name, though not always by nature.'

She did not seem to think that at all funny. 'My name's Mrs Archer,' she said. 'The girls are expecting you. At least, Debbie is. Vicky has just popped out for a minute. Come on through. May I take your coats?'

She chattered on about the weather, the traffic, the problems of getting taxis, the cost of things.

In the sitting room, a small, pale girl was curled up in one of the armchairs, embroidering. She looked like someone's secretary having a quiet evening in – so much so that I couldn't help wondering if we hadn't blundered into someone's home.

Mrs Archer said, 'Debbie, offer our guests a drink. Or perhaps you'd prefer tea or coffee?'

Wishing at all events to keep a clear head, I said that a cup of coffee would suit me very well.

'My friend leads a very sheltered life,' said Beddoes. 'Unlike me, I'm afraid.' He laughed loudly. 'A large whisky and soda for me if you please, with ice, but easy on the soda.'

Debbie said, 'It makes a change to meet someone who doesn't drink.' And she disappeared into the kitchen.

Though far from being my type, Debbie looked very much a girl who would understand the sort of thing I was after, so decided to make my position clear straight away.

Slipped out of the room, closing the door behind me. Hurried along passage and into kitchen where Debbie was laying up a tray with cups, sugar bowl, coffee pot, After Eight Mints, etc.

I said it was all very different from what I'd been expecting.

She said, 'Is this your first time?'

I replied with a laugh, 'First and last, I hope. I'm not your average client, you know.'

She said, 'Oh really?'

'Good Lord, no,' I said. 'I'm here for a very special reason. I expect Beddoes mentioned something about it on the phone.'

'No,' said Debbie. 'He didn't. What sort of special reason?'

I said, 'Oh it's really very straightforward. You're obviously an intelligent girl. I think you'll find you'll be able to give me everything I need.'

She said rather nervously, 'That depends. I don't go in for dressing up or S & M or anything like that.'

Clearly some sort of interpreter was called for. Luckily, at that moment Beddoes appeared in the doorway.

'Hallo, hallo,' he said suggestively. 'What are you two love-birds up to then? Happy families in the kitchen, is it?'

Seizing him by the arm, I manoeuvred him back into the sitting room. 'Someone's lines appear to have become crossed somewhere,' I said, and described the curious turn our apparently simple conversation had so abruptly taken.

Beddoes said, 'Leave it to me, laddie.'

A moment or two later, the two of them returned, giggling like a couple of naughty children.

'I think Debbie understands what you have in mind now,' said Beddoes, and they both giggled even harder. I couldn't see the joke myself.

Eventually Debbie pulled herself together sufficiently to pour me a cup of black coffee and offer me an After Eight.

'Would you like to watch some TV?' she said.

Naturally assumed that what she *really* meant was, did I want to watch one of the pornographic tapes which I've heard they keep handy in this sort of place to help nervous customers get more sexed up. I replied by way of an in-joke that in my view there was never very much to watch on telly on Friday nights.

Beddoes said that, in the continuing absence of Vicky, he wouldn't mind looking in for a while.

'Tape or live?' Debbie asked.

'Tape for me every time,' said Beddoes, 'I like to live dangerously.'

While she was selecting something suitable, I slipped next door for a quick wash and brush-up. Returned a couple of minutes later to find Debbie gone and Beddoes, with another large whisky and soda in one hand and a cheroot in the other, watching Sir Huw Weldon examining a large, elaborately carved piece of furniture.

I said, 'I never knew Huw Weldon went in for this sort of thing.'

'What sort of thing?' he said. 'This is *Royal Heritage*. Charles II and the later Stuarts. I missed this particular one the first time round. Look at that carving.'

By an odd coincidence, the Charles II programme had somehow eluded me too, and I had given up all hope of ever seeing it. However, had no sooner settled down with a second cup of coffee and another After Eight than Debbie stuck her head round the door and announced that she was ready if I was, and that Vicky was back.

Suggested to Beddoes that he watch something else for the time being and that we watch *Royal Heritage* together later.

He replied that there might not be a later and that he had always believed that, unless one seized the moment in this life, one invariably regretted it. 'I suggest you seize yours,' he said, 'and I'll seize mine.'

Marched purposefully towards the door and pulled it open to find myself face to face with our old flatmate Victoria. Was so astounded, all I could think of saying was, 'What in the world are you doing here?'

She replied coolly, 'I might ask you the same thing.'

I said, 'I'm researching.'

'I might have guessed it,' she said. 'Well, I work here.'

Assumed at first that this was all an elaborate plot dreamed up by Beddoes, but obviously he was as taken aback as I was.

She told us that things hadn't worked out between her and Mike Pritchard, thanks largely to the very attack of alopecia that had sent Victoria rushing from my side to his last spring.

'It was like Samson and Delilah,' she said. 'With his hair went his strength, if you see what I mean. In the end he became so depressed he went back to Babs and the children. He's a producer with local radio somewhere in the north. The kids call him Radio Savalas.'

I said that was all very unfortunate but that still did not explain how she came to be doing what she was.

'It happens,' she said. 'Actually, for the first time in my life I've found my true métier.'

I said, 'But I thought your great aim in life was putting the world to rights.'

'It still is,' she said. 'Only now I tackle the problems in a more personal way. How can man hope to be free until he throws off his sexual shackles? I see myself as the first truly left-wing sex therapist. It's extremely satisfying, I can tell you. For all concerned.'

Beddoes, who has to make a joke of everything, said, 'Funnily enough, I've been suffering from a rather embarrassing complaint myself recently.' And he put his arm suggestively round Victoria's waist. 'Your place or yours?' he said, leering horribly.

Victoria extracted herself neatly from his fumbling embrace. 'I'm sorry,' she said, suddenly serious. 'I couldn't possibly go with either of you. It would be quite out of the question.'

Beddoes said, 'You're joking. Not even for old time's sake?'

'Especially not for that,' she said.

I said, 'I suggest that in the circumstances we call it a day. It's all been most interesting and I think I've certainly got enough to be getting on with.'

Beddoes said, 'You may have. I certainly haven't.'

I said, 'The trouble with you, Beddoes, is that you never know where to draw the line. Now then, how much do we owe you girls for your time?'

Beddoes continued to complain in a facetious way, but the girls' attention was by now firmly fixed on the question of money.

Debbie said, 'That's up to you.'

I said, 'Would twenty cover it?'

'Twenty each?' said Victoria.

'Good heavens no,' I said. 'Between you. I'm not made of money.'

'You must be joking,' she said.

'How much then?' I said.

She said, 'Most punters wouldn't expect to get out under a hundred.'

Felt myself go quite weak at the knees. I said, 'But we didn't actually, you know . . .'

She said, 'That was your choice, not ours.'

I said that I would have thought that chatting was a good deal less wearing and should therefore be charged at a considerably lower rate.

Victoria said, 'It may be less wearing for you, but as far as we're concerned, it's merely another way of taking advantage of our experience and, if anything, it takes longer.'

Beddoes said, 'In that case, I'm certainly going to have my money's worth.' And before I could stop him he had grabbed the unfortunate Debbie and marched off down the passage with her.

I said to Victoria, 'I expect you're used to this sort of behaviour.'

She said, 'All punters are the same, and as far as I'm concerned, Beddoes is just another punter.'

I said, 'That hardly sounds like the tart with the heart of gold.'

'Can't afford to be,' she said. 'I've got a living to make.'

I said, 'I know what you mean. I could never really be a punter.'

She said, 'Either you are or you aren't. Some people are doers; you just like talking about it. You were always like that in the flat and you haven't changed.'

I wasn't about to have her taking a high moral tone with me. I said, 'I happen to be doing my job. I suppose that next you'll be trying to tell me the Deputy Managing Director of Barfords is a secret voyeur.'

'Keith Hardacre?' she said. 'I know bloody well he is. He's one of my oldest clients.'

For only the second time in my life, rendered utterly speechless. Unfortunately, before I could recover sufficiently to press Victoria for further information, Beddoes came marching along the passage, very red in the face, pulling on his jacket, and pursued by an anxious-looking Debbie.

'This is the last time I do you a favour,' he shouted.

When I asked him what on earth he was talking about, all he would say was, 'Ask her.' And he pointed at Debbie.

'It's no good,' she said, her eyes brimming with tears. 'I can't manage with people I fancy.'

'Excuses, excuses,' muttered Beddoes.

I said, 'But you ought to be flattered.'

'Flattered?' he shouted. 'Who needs flattery? I can get that any day of the week for nothing.' And still shouting, he marched out of the front door.

Decided the only way to defuse the situation was to pay up as quickly as possible and leave. Unfortunately, American Express card not received quite as graciously as in the TV ads. I had a good mind to tell Hardacre to settle up the next time he was round, but in the end the girls settled for a personal cheque.

I said to Victoria, 'See you again one of these days perhaps.'

'I doubt it,' she said.

So do I somehow. Business and pleasure make uneasy bedfellows.

Beddoes silent and bad-tempered all the way home in the taxi. I should have thought if anyone had a grudge to bear, it was me against him.

Still, it shouldn't be too difficult to get my £200 refunded, knowing what I now do about Keith Hardacre's extra-curricular activities. But the trousers, though old, are irreplaceable.

Saturday

An anxious afternoon of indecision while Beddoes tried to make up his mind whether or not to visit parents in Gravesend.

Unfortunately, made cardinal error of letting slip about Sue's party, and from then on there was no getting rid of him. Nor of making any useful progress re putting my notes in coherent shape.

In the end, felt duty bound to ring Sue and explain dilemma. Painted Beddoes in worst light possible.

'He sounds fun,' she said. 'Bring him along.'

I pointed out that he would almost certainly behave badly.

'That's what parties are for, isn't it?' she said.

For some, perhaps. The moment we arrived I knew I had made a terrible mistake. Music too loud, people too young, food too unpalatable, drink too undrinkable, Sue too taken up with her chums even to look at me.

Decided the only solution was to use the event as the basis for my Sex Among Flatsharers section, and wandered about, notebook and pencil in hand, observing.

Beddoes clearly in his element, since every time I saw him he was on his way into or out of one of the bedrooms and each time with a different girl.

For some reason was reminded of an incident that occurred in a flat I once shared in the sixties. Was smiling fondly at the memory of those far-off golden days when I was aware of a girl standing looking at me and saying something. 'What?' I said.

She said, 'I said a penny for them.'

I smiled and shook my head. 'You wouldn't understand.'

'Try me,' she said.

She had such a pretty smile that I did as she asked. She listened most attentively and when I got to the bit about the sheets, she said, 'Is that it?'

I said, 'I told you you wouldn't understand. I don't suppose you've heard of Profumo either, or Christine Keeler, or the Cuban missile crisis, or Freddie and the Dreamers.'

She said, 'I remember my parents talking about someone

called Christine Keeler. Wasn't she a famous tennis player?'

It was like talking to Amanda Trubshawe all over again. Of course, I should have recognized the warning lights straight away and left at once, but was so delighted at finding a captive subject at last, my only thought was to get her into a quiet corner and pump her for information.

I said, 'Is there a quiet room where we could go?'

Unhappily, she got quite the wrong end of the stick and before I knew what, I was grappling with her amongst a pile of coats on a mattress on the spare room floor.

'I hope you don't mind,' she panted. 'I'm a very physical person.'

I said that I was pretty robust myself – under normal circumstances.

'You can't get circumstances more normal than these,' she muttered, and rolled onto her back, pulling me hard on top of her. As she did so, my notebook and pencil fell out of my hand and disappeared among the coats. Anxious to recover them at once before they became lost for ever, I leaned over and scrabbled around with my left hand.

At that moment, my neck went.

'That's it,' I said. 'My neck's gone stiff.'

'It's the only thing that has,' said the girl.

She stood up. 'My mother was right,' she said. 'You're all the same, you middle-aged guys. Tired in the evening, hungry in the daytime and randy in the morning.'

And with that she left the room, slamming the door and leaving me in the dark, searching for my precious notes.

Located them but not Beddoes. Left him to get on with it and drove home. Very slowly.

Sunday

A wretched night. Neck so bad, unable to move an inch without great pain. So terrified Beddoes might come back at any minute and ring the front door bell, that didn't get a wink all night.

Spent morning with papers. Neck slightly easier after bout of self-manipulation in bath.

Even so, did not wish to risk muscle spasm with large movements of the arms, etc., so for the first time for years bought *Mirror* and *People* instead of usual heavies. And thank heavens I did. For what should I come across but a fascinating exposé of the fast-growing British craze for striptease? It seems that while audiences have been declining in Soho, due to the high prices, elsewhere in Britain, in pubs, at cricket and rugger club dinners, stag nights, even business conferences, a striptease act is now considered very much an accepted part of the proceedings.

Feel this is definitely something that needs investigating. I have been concentrating far too heavily on London and the Home Counties, and a brief visit to the provinces can only help to add an extra dimension to my study. By a lucky coincidence, am due to go to Manchester with Pratt on Wednesday to give a talk to our northern salesmen about my New York trip and the Kellerman contract.

Must try to arrange for us to take in a Mancunian strip club or two while we are there. Pratt will probably be only too delighted and we can put it on his expenses.

Speaking of which, have at last itemized my exes to date:

	£
Adult films	9.00
Theatres	9.50
Magazines	8.00
Sex shop goods	15.00
Time Out advertisement	14.90
Lunches with various experts	80.00
Taxis/transport	30.00
Refreshments (sundry)	25.00
Sundry expenses incurred during interviews/research etc.	250.00
	441.40

I do not believe anyone could complain about that. Sex is an expensive business these days, as Hardacre should know!

Beddoes finally deigned to roll in just after lunch, looking far too pleased with himself for my liking.

'What happened to you?' he said. He indicated my surgical collar. 'Trying out a few new positions, were you?'

'Only one,' I said. 'It's called lowering oneself to other people's level.'

He said, 'You have a positive talent for leaving at just the wrong moment.'

'Some of us,' I said, 'can tell the difference between right and wrong.'

He went on, 'You go round for weeks searching in vain for an orgy, and yet you can't see one when it comes up and hits you between the eyes.'

Apparently things did get out of hand last night, as I thought they might; marks were overstepped and lines not drawn.

Beddoes elaborated, 'It wasn't until that boyfriend of Sue's appeared that things really started to warm up.'

'Boyfriend?' I said.

'Chappie she works for in your office,' Beddoes said. 'Begins with a T, I think.'

'Pratt?' I said.

'I thought so,' said Beddoes. 'But what imagination!'

I doubt if I have ever felt more wretched than I did at that moment.

Beddoes said, 'Cheer up. It may never happen.' Then he added with a laugh, 'It hasn't so far anyway.'

I said, 'I thought you were going to Gravesend.'

He looked at his watch. 'It hardly seems worth it now,' he said.

I said, 'In that case, I wonder if you'd mind awfully going back to Belgium.'

'My flight's not till ten,' he said.

I said, 'You've managed to occupy yourself perfectly well so far today; I'm sure you'll be able to think up something equally amusing for the remaining few hours of your stay. Goodbye, and I suggest that next time you fancy a weekend in London, you book into a hotel. That's obviously where you think you've been for the last few days.'

At that, I rose and left the room in dignified silence, but caught the pocket of my sports jacket on the door handle as I did so, giving it a slight tear.

Went to my room, closed the door firmly behind me and locked it.

Heard Beddoes pottering about uncertainly for a few minutes. He then went into his room, pottered about some more and then came along the passage. He paused outside my door. 'I'll be off then, laddie,' he said. 'See you anon when you're in a better mood. You probably need a few early nights. And a bottle or two of Sanatogen. Money's on the table.'

The moment the front door had closed, hurried back into the sitting room, catching my other pocket as I did so, and there on the table, propped up against the vase of dried flowers, was an envelope with my name on it. Inside were five twenty-pound notes. Have not as yet made up my mind whether to keep them.

Took a couple of Veganin and spent the rest of the afternoon in bed, trying not to think about anything or anybody.

Got up at seven, bathed, got into my pyjamas and dressing gown, and was just settling down in front of the TV with a plate of scrambled eggs and Penelope Keith when the phone went.

It was Vanessa Pedalow in floods of tears, saying that Tim had left her again, this time for good, and could she see me.

Must admit that, amused as I generally am by the Pedalows, my heart sank. Guessed it would take her at least half an hour to get to me, so that at least I wouldn't have to miss Penelope and the detective series. I said, 'See you here in about half an hour then.'

She said, 'Tim's taken the BMW and the Mini's on the blink. I'll never get a taxi round here at this time on a Sunday evening. You couldn't possibly be an angel and come and fetch me, could you?'

Wouldn't have minded turning out quite so much if I had been able to move my head while driving. Vanessa, however, so taken up with her own tale of woes, she did not appear to notice anything amiss, despite several heavy hints.

Barely had we got into the flat than she said, 'Something smells delicious.'

I said it was only scrambled eggs on toast.

'Only!' she exclaimed. 'I'd give my right arm for a plate of eggs – scrambled, poached, anything.'

I said, 'I think there's only one left.'

I was going to add that I was keeping it for breakfast, but before I could get the words out, she said, 'I don't mind.

I'm not greedy. It's just that, what with one thing and another, I haven't eaten all day.'

When she had polished off my last egg, my last two slices of bread and my last drop of milk, she launched into a long and involved account of Tim's latest sexual escapade. It appeared to involve the wife of his oldest friend and represented, according to Vanessa, the end of the line as far as she and Tim were concerned.

'Goodness knows what he sees in her,' she said.

Never having clapped eyes on the lady in question but keen to help, I made a few stabs in the dark.

'Perhaps,' I said, 'he's going through an early middle-age crisis and she seems to represent something in his life which he feels, quite wrongly I'm sure, that you cannot provide.'

'Such as?' she said, rather snappily.

'I've no idea,' I said. 'Perhaps she just feels sorry for him. Or vice versa.'

'Balls,' said Vanessa. 'She's got big boobs, that's all.'

'Aha,' I said. 'So you think sex is at the bottom of it?'

'Isn't it always?' she said.

I said, 'But I thought you had both taken up this new celibacy thing one hears is sweeping across the western world.'

Vanessa said, 'It's certainly swept through our little corner of it, I can tell you. Mainly since Tim took up with this stupid girl.'

'But I'd always thought you two enjoyed a full and active sex life,' I said.

She said, 'It depends on what you call full and active. I'm always reading articles in the newspapers that talk about couples making love two and a half times a week on average. I'm jolly grateful if we manage it once every three months.'

If what Vanessa had told me was a true representation of the sex life of the average thirty-five to forty-year-old professional married couple, then I was on to something which, if published, could set the whole world of sociology by the ears and rock the very foundations of middle-class life in Britain today.

I said to her, 'Would you be prepared to give me a long, searching interview on the subject?'

She said, 'The way I'm feeling right now, I'd be prepared to have an affair with you.'

I laughed and said, 'No, seriously, Vanessa, would you?'

'Have an affair with you?' she said. 'Why not? Why should I be the one to miss out on all the fun?'

Having never been on the receiving end of a proposition of this kind from a married woman before, was not quite sure how to react. I must admit I have always secretly had a soft spot for Vanessa. She is a little tall for my liking and her manner can be rather on the sharp side, but in many ways she is very much my type.

I told her that I was as familiar with the way the world wagged as the next man, but that I was not used to going in for this sort of thing in quite such a matter-of-fact sort of way.

'Me neither,' she said. 'But frankly I'm sick to death of all this open-mindedness and mutual understanding that goes with modern adultery. One's natural reaction is not to go rushing straight home and confess all, but to carry on sneakily behind the other one's back and hope they never find out. That's what gives the whole thing its spice. Elaborate plans, elaborate excuses, coded telephone calls, cheap hotel rooms, Mr and Mrs Smith, dark glasses, slouch hats: adultery as it always used to be and as it should be. That's what I'm in the mood for right now. If you don't fancy it, you only have to say so.'

I said, 'Well, if you think it'll be all right. Where did you have in mind? Here? Now?'

'Good Lord, no,' she said. 'It's got to be somewhere with a warm, cosy atmosphere. This place is about as sexy as a Borstal.'

She went on to explain that she had some friends with a flat in Mayfair, just off Curzon Street. They were away in California at the moment and had left her the key and asked her to look after it for them. She said that it was the perfect setting for an affair – nice and central, well-heated and furnished, and the chances of running into Tim in that area were remote.

She added, 'I always think these things go better on neutral ground, don't you?'

I've no idea. All I know is that somehow or other I have

agreed to spend the night with her there on Tuesday.

Sorry to have missed Penelope Keith.

Monday, 19 February

A restless night, filled with erotic dreams involving Jane, of all people. In one, we were in an enormous penthouse suite on top of the Dorchester Hotel, about to get busy on a centrally heated circular bed when Tim appeared in the room, disguised as a waiter, and broke my neck.

Woke up in even greater agony than last night.

Great excitement at breakfast. The Thruster has arrived at last. It is rather like a solid cricket box which you simply tie inside your underpants and 'wait for the incredible reactions which are sure to follow'.

Decided not to wear it to work. All my trousers are really too loose-fitting for the effect to be fully appreciated.

However, took it with me in briefcase and en route slipped into boutique and bought myself tightest pair of corduroy trousers I could get into. Slightly alarmed to note that right thigh soon went quite numb, but assistant said that was normal with people with 34-inch waists who try to squeeze into 32-inch trousers and that, as soon as the waistband had begun to stretch, the circulation would quickly return. He also suggested I give up underpants in favour of briefs.

To gents immediately on arrival in office to insert Thruster. Am quite relieved I am not better equipped in biological sense.

Had not realized lump would be quite so prominent. However, there's no doubt it gives one a certain *je ne sais quoi*, and I found myself walking along corridor with a decidedly jaunty gait, even though to and fro movements of legs rather more constricted than usual.

Passed several secretaries on the way and made a point of stopping and chatting to them about this and that. I think they must have been so nervous at being spoken to by an executive of my level that they never even noticed.

Strode into office feeling like Clint Eastwood. Sue already at desk and on phone – to Pratt no doubt, mulling over happy memories of Saturday night. Gave her a cold stare and marched through to inner sanctum.

Unfortunately, unable to sit down without extreme discomfort, so perched nonchalantly on edge of desk and waited. By the time Sue eventually appeared, bottom as sore as everything else.

Dictated a few letters etc., but made no reference to Saturday night's activities, nor to Thruster. Nor, I'm sorry to say, did she. She is going on the principle, presumably, that silence implies innocence.

I wasn't having any of that, and announced in a loud voice that I was just going to the third floor to see Pratt. I pronounced his name with special emphasis.

'Right,' she said, and didn't even look up.

Strolled up and down various corridors for several minutes but unable to provoke the slightest reaction from anyone. Perhaps people take it for granted that this is the natural result of wearing very tight-fitting trousers. Like ballet dancers in their tights.

Arrived back at office to be told by Sue that I had a visitor. Went through to find the chairman's secretary, Erica, sitting in my swivel chair, thumbing through one of my contact magazines.

She said gaily, 'I hope you don't mind. I was looking for a piece of paper to write you a note, opened the first drawer to hand and found these. I would never have guessed this was your sort of thing.'

I said, 'It isn't actually,' and went on to explain what I was up to.

She said, 'Why didn't you come and ask me? I could have told you all you need to know.'

Was so relieved I burst out laughing. 'That's wonderful,' I said. 'When can I come and talk to you?'

She said, 'Any time you like. I'm just off skiing in America for three weeks. They say people really swing in those Rockies resorts. Shall we say about mid-March?'

As she was leaving, she turned and said, 'There's something different about you. Don't tell me.' She stared at me for a moment, then said, 'I know what it is. You've got fatter.'

I suppose she is the expert on swapping etc. she claims to be – though a girl who can seriously put a large weasel down to overeating cannot altogether be trusted to know what's what.

Passed several more people on way to coffee machine and back but still no reaction. Decided the time had come to bring things to a head. Marched up to Sue's desk and asked her straight out if there was anything about me she'd noticed.

She said, 'Your trousers are two sizes too small. A man in your position ought to be able to afford properly cut clothes.'

'Anything else?' I said.

She looked me up and down. 'Not really,' she said. 'Apart from whatever it is you've pushed inside your flies.'

To Harley Preston after lunch, in Thruster, for meeting about Manchester Regional Sales Conference.

Ruth looking softer and more feminine than I have ever seen her. She must be in love. Decided this was as good a moment as any to bury the hatchet, and began by giving her one of my beaming smiles.

'May I say,' I said, 'how very pretty you're looking today, Miss Macmichael?'

'Never mind all that,' she said. 'I met a friend of yours on Friday. Name of Ralph Beddoes. He doesn't hang about, does he?'

I said, 'Don't tell me you actually fell for that brutish English male-chauvinist charm?'

'There are,' she said, 'male chauvinists and male chauvinists. Naturally, I could never consider any serious long-term relationship with a man like that, but for a one off I've got no complaints. Sex in the afternoon has a charm all of its own.'

I don't think I've ever seen her looking quite so excited about anything.

I said, rather pointedly, 'Well, as long as you enjoyed yourselves, that's the main thing, isn't it?'

'We certainly did,' she said. 'My God, your apartment's uncomfortable though.'

The meeting went extraordinarily smoothly considering, and everyone seemed to think my speech fitted the bill very nicely. Even Ruth had only two criticisms to make – both levelled, as usual, against my use of humour.

As I sat down afterwards, felt something give in my waistband, but assumed this to be part of stretching process and thought no more about it.

Later, we came to the section dealing with the presentation of sales charts.

A very odd thing happened. Was on the point of running through them for third time, when suddenly Roundtree came across carrying a chair and asked if I'd prefer to sit down. I said that I was perfectly happy standing.

'Are you sure?' he said.

'Perfectly thank you, Roundtree,' I said.

Afterwards, he came up to me, I thought to congratulate me. Instead, he took me to one side and asked if I was sure I was up to the presentation.

I said, 'Why? Are the figures still confusing?'

'No, no,' he said. 'Physically I mean. That leg of yours. It looks so painful. Water on the knee, is it?'

I looked down to discover that my knee had indeed swelled horribly. In panic, seized it in both hands and suddenly realized that what I was holding was the Thruster. Thank heaven for tight trousers, otherwise it might have slipped right down to the floor.

I straightened up, looked Roundtree firmly in the eye and said in a loud voice, 'It's kind of you to ask, Roundtree, but it's nothing. An old skiing accident. Lauberhorn actually. Years ago now, but it can blow up in the cold weather. I've got used to it, I hardly ever notice it.'

And limping slightly, I left the room.

Tuesday

Woke early with sinking feeling in pit of stomach. For a moment or two could not think why, then suddenly remembered today was the day I was due to start my affair with Vanessa Pedalow.

At all events, it's bound to be interesting, and I'm still very short of stuff for my adultery section.

After breakfast, packed a small overnight bag. Toothbrush, shaving tackle, flannel, brush and comb etc. a must, of course, but would one be able to use these people's towels? And how about dressing gown and slippers in case one wanted to sit about and chat over a drink during a refreshment break? And pyjamas? Have tried on occasions sleeping in the nude, but it has never been a great success, owing to the fact that I spend all night dreaming I am wandering around the streets without any clothes on and wake up feeling exhausted. Also, one never knows how well off people are for blankets. In the end, settled for a neat compromise by slipping in a T-shirt, just in case. I read somewhere that they're rather a turn-on for certain types of girls.

My biggest headache, though, (or should I say neck-ache?) is my soft collar. My neck, though definitely improving, is by no means 100 per cent and, if I don't wear my collar at night, I could undo all the good work to date. A difficult decision, but on balance would prefer to lose Vanessa than another cervical disc.

My attention so taken up with tonight's adventure that was scarcely able to concentrate on anything else all day.

I'm afraid that, when Bryant-Fenn rang this morning to say when were we having our lunch, I gave him very short change indeed. Have agreed to meet him at 1.15 tomorrow at this new French place in Covent Garden everyone keeps banging on about.

Pratt called in on the pretence of wanting to check some last-minute figures for Friday, but I'm too old a campaigner to be taken in by that sort of ploy. As he was leaving, I said, in a loud voice, 'How's your love life these days, Neville?' Of course he pretended innocence. He must take me for a bloody fool.

Could not resist a little dig at Sue as I was leaving. 'Enjoyed the do the other night,' I said casually. 'Sorry I had to leave early. Had to be up early in the morning. Pressure of work, you know.'

She said, 'Yes, I'm sorry we didn't have a chance to chat. You know what it's like at one's own party. Pity you couldn't have stayed a few more minutes. Things really livened up.'

'So I heard,' I said, raised my eyebrows suggestively, and left.

Met Vanessa in small Italian restaurant near Grosvenor Square, as arranged. Amused to note she was wearing sunglasses, even though lighting in restaurant very subdued.

I said, 'I like your disguise.'

She said, 'Actually, I've got pinkeye and it's extremely painful.'

Somehow struggled through a plate of saltimbocca, half a carafe of red wine and some desultory conversation, but my eye more on door than on table. I've known Vanessa to be better company, too.

Finally, paid our bill, sneaked out into street, and began to walk down South Audley Street. I do not think I have felt less like having an affair in my life.

'Isn't this fun?' I said.

'No,' she said.

Blocks of flats newer and smarter than I had imagined – just behind Hilton. I don't think anyone saw us going in. Anyway, it's always difficult to recognize someone when he has an overcoat over his head.

Hurried into lift. Vanessa pressed one of the buttons and soon we were standing in thick pile carpet outside solid-looking pine door. I do not believe I have ever seen quite so many locks and anti-burglar devices in my life.

Flat small, neat and furnished in a mixture of modern and traditional styles. Procter prints, drink bottles in antique baby's cradle, etc. It was like walking into a *Sunday Times Colour Magazine*.

Went to kiss Vanessa who said, 'I'm convinced that at any moment the front door is going to open and Bill and Lucy are going to walk in.'

I said, 'But I thought you said they were in California.'

'They are,' she said, 'but what guarantee's that?'

I said, 'Why don't we lock all the doors and set the burglar alarm, and then if Bill and Lucy do come back unexpectedly, we'll have time to get up and get dressed while they're unravelling it all.'

Quickly undressed and put on T-shirt, dressing gown and slippers, and cleaned teeth. Came back into sitting room just as Vanessa was putting last touches to burglar alarm.

We were halfway through *News at Ten* and our whisky and sodas when she remembered she'd left all her night creams in a vanity case in the boot of the car.

I said I'd go and went to unlock front door, but without success. Vanessa became rather irritable at this and launched into a long attack on men's inability to do any-thing when it was really needed. Delighted, therefore, when she, too, unable to crack locks.

Slightly less delighted when, after half an hour's combined struggling, it became clear that we were going to have to ring for the porter.

In our anxiety to escape, it had slipped our minds that we were both moderately déshabillés, with the result that the porter arrived to find us still struggling into our day clothes and we had to buy his silence with a tenner. Since I was now out of pocket completely, Vanessa compelled to drive me home in the Mini. I asked if she'd like to carry on where we'd left off in my flat, but she said that enough was quite enough for one day – perhaps another time.

To judge from this evening's events, adultery not quite all it's cracked up to be. On the other hand, we had probably got to know each other better through adversity than we would have done through straightforward Coleman, and actually my neck is really not yet up to coping with unknown pillows.

To bed in cheerful mood.

Wednesday

As I travelled in to work this morning, could not help looking about me at my fellow passengers and wondering how many of them had ever tried adultery and, if so, whether they had had better luck with it than I had. Cannot say that many of them looked the type. But then, who does?

Just as one cannot imagine one's parents getting down to a spot of uninhibited hanky-panky, so one cannot really believe that most people one sees have ever entertained a rude thought or indulged in saucy behaviour in their lives.

Of course, there are always exceptions, one of them being Sue. Am still haunted by a mental image of her, Pratt and Beddoes rolling around among the coats in the spare room in her flat. Cannot make up my mind whether I am more or less keen on her as a result. All I do know is that her presence in the outer office is extremely disturbing. For two pins would suggest having her removed to another part of the building were it not for the fact that, with less than a week to go, she still hasn't begun typing up the report.

As soon as I arrived this morning, therefore, suggested

she make a start on the sex film section. Have told her there's plenty more where that came from.

Is it my imagination, or has a new note of respect crept into her voice? Perhaps I should have brought her to heel a long time ago.

Sent off my expenses to Hardacre with a covering memo.

Memo: Private and Confidential

From: Simon Crisp
To: Keith Hardacre   21 February

Herewith my expenses, as discussed. I think you'll agree they're modest enough.

When one is asked to deal with a subject as wide-ranging as this, one is bound to run up against the odd snag. If I am to do full justice to this survey, and thus to Barfords' public image, I shall need to extend the deadline by a few days, especially since I have had to take time off for this Manchester presentation.

I feel sure you will agree.

Vicky sends her love. Need I say more?

S.C.

Met Bryant-Fenn at 1.15 as agreed. Restaurant done up in style of old-fashioned French brasserie. Hugh just polishing off large *pastis* as I arrived.

He said, 'This couldn't suit me better. I've been meaning to write the place up for my column for weeks. Trouble is, I've been rather overspending on my budget recently, so your invitation came like a lifeboat to a drowning man.'

About to point out that he had invited himself, but when you're in the position of having to get a lot of information out of someone in a very short space of time, you take care not to rock the boat.

Cannot imagine that the readers of *Bedroom* magazine rate high among the world's gastronomes, but that did not deter Bryant-Fenn from ordering the most expensive things on the menu. My onion soup, though at £1.80 it undoubtedly helped to counterbalance his smoked salmon stuffed with lobster at £4.50, tasted every bit as uninspiring as it looked.

Hugh said, 'This smoked salmon is out of this world. Your soup looks dull.'

I said, 'It is rather. Perhaps I could have a taste of yours?'

'If there's one thing I can't bear in restaurants,' he said, 'it's people who choose badly and then try to compensate by picking at others' food.'

Was not about to make the same mistake twice, so announced that I wished to change my tournedos for something rather more exotic.

Hugh said, 'Why not try the calves' brains? It would help me if you had something typically French. I think you'll find it rather amusing and it'll go very well with this excellent Bordeaux.'

I do not believe I have ever had a more unappetizing plate of food placed before me in my life. Calves' brains are certainly no joke to my way of thinking.

'Anything the matter?' said Hugh, tucking into his *filet de boeuf*.

I said, 'Actually, I've rather lost my appetite.'

'You know why, don't you?' he said. 'You shouldn't have had that onion soup. It's far too filling.' And he launched into a long boring monologue about proteins and carbohydrates and polyunsaturates.

Tried on several occasions to bend the conversation to figures and thence to girlie magazines, but without success.

Finally, over the cognac and coffee, I said that, to judge from the letters I have been reading in *Bedroom* and similar publications, his readers had appetites of a quite different kind.

'Really?' said Hugh. 'I wouldn't know about that. I only ever read my own columns.'

I said, 'But what about your competitors? *Penthouse*, *Men Only*, *Whitehouse* and so on.'

Hugh said, 'I've no idea. I never look at them.'

I said, 'But I thought you told me you were an expert on this sort of thing?'

'Did I?' he said. 'I can't think why. Perhaps it was a joke.'

I replied that our lunch certainly hadn't been a joke.

He said, 'I quite agree. They run a pretty serious kitchen here. I'm so glad you brought me. It saved my life. Must dash. May I leave you to deal with *l'addition*?' And without so much as an apology he stood up and walked out of the door.

L'addition came to just under £50!

Rang Vanessa as soon as I got back to the office to explain that I had had second thoughts re our affair, but somehow or other I seem to have agreed to try again, same time, same place tomorrow night.

Does too much sex soften the brain, I ask myself?

Thursday

Bryant-Fenn rang this morning. Assumed it was to apologize for not keeping his side of the bargain in the matter of the lunch, but, as usual, I overestimated his finer feelings.

He said, 'The thing is, as you may know, I've recently started handling the public relations for Dorothy.'

'Who's she?' I said. 'A pop singer?'

Hugh tutted irritably. 'Dorothy,' he said. 'You know, the new niterie in Kensington High Street. Bianca Jagger and all that. I was wondering if you'd be interested in coming along one evening and having a look – on the house. Come Saturday; there should be some big names about. Bianca mentioned something about looking in. You could talk to her. I'll be there. Shall we say about ten, in the bar? Bring someone if you want.' And he rang off.

I may take him up on his offer or I may not. Have always been rather curious to see what goes on in these places and, knowing the sort of prices they charge for membership, it's unlikely that the opportunity will occur again in the near future. Oddly enough, have always been rather keen on Bianca. If I do go, shall almost certainly not take a companion.

A memo arrived from Hardacre this afternoon.

Memo

From: Keith Hardacre
To: Simon Crisp   22 February

Subject: *Sex Report*

I disagree. Your expenses are far higher than I'd hoped or

expected. It is really necessary to go *everywhere* by taxi? As for the £200, said to cover 'sundry expenses', I couldn't possibly sanction this without some sort of breakdown.

Re completion date. I'm afraid I cannot allow any extension on this.

Good luck with the Manchester presentation, and please return my love to Vicky next time you see her.

KH

The older I become, the more convinced I am that I am not made for the cut and thrust of big business. Or for blackmail apparently.

Vanessa rang to say that her Mini had conked out again and could I pick her up from the San Frediano at 10.30.

Washed a few smalls, hoovered right through, packed a small holdall with shaving tackle, notes for speech, etc, and arrived at San Fred to find her standing just inside doorway, looking decidedly cross.

She said, 'You took your time.'

Pointed out that, according to my watch, it was exactly 10.30.

She said, 'You do take life literally.'

That may or may not be so, but I do object to being treated like a husband before I have even become a lover.

As we drove up the Brompton Road, she snuggled up against my arm and said in a lovey-dovey voice, 'Don't you want to know who I've been having dinner with?'

'Not specially,' I said.

'Of course you do,' she said. 'Well, if you must know, it was Tim.'

I nearly drove off the road.

'It's all right,' she said. 'I told him I was having an affair, but didn't mention your name.'

Am not sure whether to take this as a compliment or not.

Since I would be away the whole of the next day, decided to put the car in a garage and be done with it.

Vanessa said she would go on up to the flat with the luggage and pour drinks, etc. Suddenly realized I did not actually know flat number.

Neither, for some reason, did she. However, agreed that

she should take things up and then come down again and meet me in the lobby.

Car park slightly further away than I'd imagined. Got back to find her peering out through plate glass front doors.

She said, 'I was beginning to think you'd got cold feet.'

I laughed reassuringly and, in the lift going up, kissed her properly for the first time.

'This is more like it,' she said, and we kissed again. Confidence certainly breeds confidence.

Arrived at fourth floor to find flat door closed. 'Hallo,' I quipped. 'Is this symbolic?'

'No,' she said. 'It's bloody disastrous. I've left the keys inside.'

Pointed out that it was hardly the end of the world, since the porter obviously had a spare set.

We tried several doorbells without success and finally struck lucky on the ground floor in the shape of a man with close-cropped white hair, beard and slightly petulant voice, who told us that the porter lived in the basement in No. 2.

Hurried downstairs to find note pinned to door of porter's flat, announcing that he'd gone to stay with his sister overnight and would be back at eight the next morning.

This was a cruel blow, since my train to Manchester left just before seven and all my notes, not to say shaving tackle, clean shirt, etc., were inside the flat.

Had no alternative but to call it a day.

Got back to garage to find it locked for the night.

I said, 'Never mind. It isn't the end of the world. We'll get a taxi back to my place.'

'It may not be the end of the world,' said Vanessa, 'but it certainly is of our so-called affair. I've never had this trouble with anyone before.' And with that she hailed a passing taxi and drove off up South Audley Street.

Unfortunately, although I walked up and down for nearly half an hour, not a single free taxi came my way. Finally hailed one in Berkeley Square. Arrived home at midnight.

Was paying off the taxi when suddenly remembered I had left flat keys in car. Porter most unsympathetic. He hasn't heard the end of this by a long chalk.

Arrived at last in flat only to find I had inadvertently left electric heater full on all day. I dread to think how this could affect my quarterly bill. On the other hand, I suppose I should thank my lucky stars I caught it when I did. At least the evening was not a complete disaster.

Friday

How I do hate alarm clocks. I very rarely use them but when I do, I find I am awake every two minutes waiting for them to go off.

Woke exhausted and with splitting headache at six. Ascot heater on blink, so forced to bath in tepid water. Got out old electric shaver, plugged in and gave chin an appalling shock.

Rang all the taxi rank numbers I could find but without success. Once again forced to take to pavements.

Eventually turned up at Euston at 8.45. Absolutely no sign of Pratt. Assumed he must have gone on ahead without me, so, with sinking heart, rushed to ticket counter in hope of catching 8.55. Huge queues, needless to say.

By 8.52 had almost reached front when felt tap on shoulder. Spun round to find Pratt who said, 'Hallo, what happened to you?'

'Unexpected personal tragedy,' I said. 'I assumed you must have gone on.'

He said, 'Actually, I've only just arrived. The presentation's been put off till this afternoon. I thought we could have breakfast here and catch the 9.55. I tried to ring you at home last last night but there was no reply.'

As we were pulling out of the station, Pratt said, 'I do think you might at least have shaved.'

'I happen,' I said, 'to be growing a beard.'

'If I may say,' said Pratt, 'this kind of fringe activity would best be confined to holiday periods.'

'So, if *I* may say so,' said I, 'should inter-staff liaisons.'

As was only to be expected, Pratt pretended he had no idea what I was on about and, when I spelt it out in words of four letters, he actually claimed that he had no interest in my secretary beyond a professional one. He had never been near her flat in his life and, if ever he heard that I had been spreading rumours to the contrary, I could expect to be receiving a sharp note from his solicitor. And talking about notes, where were mine?

I replied that, like him, I found I always got away with things more easily if I played it off the cuff.

Arrived at ballroom of hotel just as salesmen were breaking off for a buffet lunch. A gloomier, more bored-looking bunch of individuals it would be hard to imagine.

Fortunately, Dave Stammers, who has just been appointed Northern Regional Manager, grabbed us and whistled us off to his private suite for champagne and smoked salmon sandwiches.

He said to me, 'You're on second from last. They'll be pretty jaded by then, so I'm relying on you to send them off in a cheerful and optimistic frame of mind. After all, if someone like you can pull off the Kellerman deal, there's hope for all of us.' He roared with laughter, slapped me on the back and poured out another glass of champagne.

Took the opportunity to question him re investigating local strip clubs for the Crisp Report. Stammers slapped me on the back yet again and poured out more champagne. 'Don't you worry about that, lad,' he said. 'It's taken care of already.'

The trouble with drinking at lunchtime is that, at the time, it slips down easily enough and it is only later that the effects begin to be felt. While I wouldn't say I was drunk exactly, by the time the proceedings were under way again at 2.15, was feeling decidedly merry.

By half past three, however, showing every sign of sobering up. Feeling in need of Dutch courage, slipped out and made my way up to Stammers' suite, where topped up liberally with Moët et Chandon Non-Vintage and arrived back much refreshed in time to hear my name being announced.

Salesmen looking even more sorry for themselves than before lunch, though not half as much as I was when I realized I couldn't remember a single word of what I had been planning to say.

Luckily, can be pretty nifty on my feet when pushed and, before I knew what, heard myself announcing that everybody took marketing far too seriously nowadays and that the sooner we put the jokes back into selling, the sooner we would have Britain back on an even keel.

I then described, rather wittily I thought, the struggle I had had with our marketing consultants over including some clips from Woody Allen films in the audio-visual part of the Kellerman presentation. The entire audience stared at me with a look of such blank incomprehension that, on an impulse, decided to give them a small taste of my famous Allen impersonation with which I used to bring the house down at Oxford parties.

It was a pity I couldn't remember it word for word, and one or two of the jokes didn't come off quite as well as they used to. However, I think the flavour came through, which is the main thing. Could have gone on for longer than I did had Stammers not jumped up on the platform and drawn things to a premature conclusion. A pity, because it brought a huge cheer.

After that, the most extraordinary thing happened. Dave gestured to me to stay where I was and, seizing the microphone, announced, 'And now, gentlemen, by special request of Mr Crisp, an extra item for your pleasure and inspiration. A young lady to show you the real meaning of figures. She's just back from Leningrad, where she was a great hit in Conservative Clubs, and last month she graced the centrefold of *Exchange and Mart*. May I present Barbara!'

The lights went out, a single spotlight was aimed at the side of the stage and, to the music of 'The Stripper', into it slinked a very pretty and curvaceous girl wearing a long dress on which were written the words: BARFORDS SALES UP 5%?

At this the entire audience burst into raucous cheers and laughter.

Barbara then proceeded to do a most seductive striptease. Each time she removed a garment she draped it over me and there was another underneath suggesting an even higher percentage, until she had no clothes on at all, whereupon she turned round and stuck out her bottom on which was printed: 30% YES!

The audience roared its approval.

She then came prancing over to me, seized her garments, tossed them to one side and, to my horror, started to undo my tie. To a man, the audience shouted, 'Get 'em off'. For an awful moment I was afraid she might take them at their word. But, of course, nothing more came of it. Barbara put a finger against my lips, seized me by the hand and dragged me off to the accompaniment of loud cheers and catcalls.

Luckily, I am the sort of man who can take a joke but, even so, the very fact that they should even contemplate such gimmicks makes me wonder if Barfords is the sort of company to which I should be making a lifetime's commitment.

Pratt came up to me afterwards and said, 'Still fancy a strip club?'

I laughed it off, but could barely bring myself to speak to him the whole way back to London. I also had one of the worst headaches of my life. My neck's much better though.

Saturday

Pretty much of a washout, thanks to continuing headache and hangover.

Vanessa rang after lunch to say she had collected the things from the flat and did I want to come round and pick them up.

I said, 'I suppose you didn't remember to pick up my car while you were about it?'

'No,' she said.

I told her I'd be round at about three.

Unfortunately, got caught up in demo round Hyde Park Corner and did not get there until nearly four.

Was waiting in hall while she went into sitting room to fetch my holdall, when a voice that I can only describe as artisan called out from upstairs, 'Are you going to be all afternoon, darling?'

Looked up to see a muscly young man in jeans and T-shirt, with curly hair and tattoos on his arms, leaning over the banisters. We stared at each other for a moment, then he withdrew as suddenly as he had appeared.

When Vanessa returned, I asked her who he was.

She said vaguely, 'Oh, he's my jobbing builder. He's come to give me an estimate for a labouring job.'

Said nothing but, if I'm not very much mistaken, there's rather more to this than meets the eye. One often hears it said that women are not averse to a spot of rough trade

116

from time to time. It will make a very telling footnote to the adultery section.

Watched *Dallas* in the evening. Am wondering if I should consider a brief comparative study of sex in the country versus sex in the city.

To Dorothy later. Bad-tempered-looking girl on door claimed never to have heard of me. Explained that I was there as a guest of Mr Bryant-Fenn.

'Who?' she said.

I repeated the name very slowly and loudly.

'Is he a member?' she said.

'He's your public relations officer,' I said. 'And, if I may say so, you are badly in need of one.'

After that, she became very rude indeed and I was forced to see the manager. A smooth-faced young man – all velvet and lace ruffles – eventually arrived and said that Hugh was not in the club and that, as far as he knew, they were not expecting him that evening.

I pointed out that I was not just anyone, but had come specially to write about them for a very important publication.

The manager shrugged. 'We've got a waiting list as long as a gorilla's arm,' he said. 'Who needs publicity? Still, if you'd like to come and have a drink and see what it's all about, you're very welcome.'

I said, 'Please don't feel you have to invite me,' in an ironic sort of way.

'Who needs *bad* publicity?' he said.

He dumped me in a large, squashy armchair in a corner of the bar and ordered me a large whisky and soda.

I declined his invitation to sample the dining room, but said that I might certainly tread a measure or two on the dance floor a little later.

He said, 'Things don't normally get going till after midnight.'

I replied that I would be quite happy to sit there soaking up the atmosphere.

'Just so long as you don't soak up the whisky,' he said, and we both laughed.

I remarked casually, 'Oh, by the way, I gather Bianca might be in this evening.'

'Who?' he said.

Spent the next couple of hours watching the so-called beautiful people at play. Some of the girls quite pretty but most of the men appeared to have been born in rather sunnier climes.

At one point, went through to next room to check action on dance floor. Only one couple caught my attention. He was tall, blond and good-looking; she was slim and graceful with straight, fairish hair. They were obviously in love.

As they came towards me, suddenly realized with a terrible shock that the girl was Amanda. Would have given anything to avoid meeting them, but she recognized me before I had a chance to move. She introduced the young man as her fiancé, name of Giles de Something.

She said to me, 'I didn't know you were a member. I've never seen you here before.'

'Nor I you,' I said blithely. 'The fact is, I don't get out much these days. I'm very busy.'

Amanda said to Giles, 'Simon is a big cheese in marketing.'

'Congratulations,' said Giles.

'Giles is a poor Army officer,' she told me.

At that moment, the barman arrived and asked us what we'd like to drink. They both looked at me. Had no option but to order. A fresh orange juice for Amanda, a large gin and tonic for Giles, and a small whisky and soda for me.

Reached in my pocket for money only to realize that I had stupidly come out without my wallet. I said in a low voice to the barman, 'I'll sign for these.'

When he handed me the bill, I wrote with a flourish across the bottom: *Hugh Bryant-Fenn*.

'Excuse me, sir,' said the barman. 'You've forgotten to add your membership number.'

At that precise moment, the manager appeared from nowhere and said, 'Don't worry, Robert. These people are with me.' And, crossing out Hugh's name, he signed his own.

'I hope you've had everything you need,' he said, putting particular emphasis on the word 'everything'.

I said I hadn't enjoyed an evening so much for a long time.

'Good,' he said. 'I'm only sorry to hear you won't be in again for a while.'

'Oh what a pity,' said Amanda. 'I was hoping to catch up on the news. Why?'

'Pressure of work,' I said. 'Please remember me to your mother.'

She said, 'I don't see her as much as I used to now that she and Daddy have split up.'

So I was right after all.

She went on, 'I wouldn't have minded if she'd found herself someone amusing. Even you would have been better than the poofy old quasi-theatrical pseud she lives with now.'

I said, 'He wouldn't happen to be called Gerald Campsey-Ash, would he?'

'Good Lord, no,' she said. 'Gerald's my uncle.'

The manager couldn't have been nicer as he accompanied me to the door.

A large car drew up as I was walking away up the road, and a young woman stepped out and walked quickly towards the door of the club.

Could have sworn I heard the manager saying, 'Bianca, darling . . .'

Sunday

Set off for Bloomsbury in good time for NACKERS meeting.

Am not quite sure what one's duties as a committee member will amount to in the months to come, but my appointment as a steward for tonight's gathering, whatever else it involved, obviously meant being there well in advance of time. Crowd handling is a tricky business, especially if one is not fully in command from the word go.

Unfortunately, experienced rather more difficulty locating hall than I had anticipated. As a result, arrived with only five minutes to spare. Place unexpectedly quiet, although fully lit. Thinking meeting must already be under way, tiptoed across lobby and in through large panelled door, only to find room completely deserted. Made my way down aisle between neatly arranged rows of wooden chairs and up on to platform.

Five minutes had passed when the door at the end of the room opened and a man in blue overalls and a peaked cap shuffled in. 'You Mr Johnson?' he called out.

I said no, but that I was expecting him any moment.

'The hall was booked for seven-thirty,' the man grumbled.

I pointed out that I happened to be a committee member and that it was only twenty to eight.

'I wouldn't care if you was Shirley Williams,' he said, 'as long as someone pays for the room and you're out of here by nine at the latest.'

By eight o'clock it was perfectly obvious that something had gone badly wrong. Unfortunately, had come out without Johnson's phone number, and no joy from Directory Enquiries.

Hung on till the bitter end, just in case, but eventually forced to admit defeat, and wrote out cheque for £25.

I'd like to know how I'm going to explain *that* on my expenses sheet.

The moment I got home, rang Howard Johnson's number but got unobtainable tone. I can't say I'm surprised. I daresay the same will hold true for my £25.

Next, rang Sue to enquire re progress of typing, only to learn that she has gone down with flu and will not be in for at least a week.

I said, 'You don't think you could do it in bed if I were to bring the material round to the flat?'

'No,' she said.

'Fair enough,' I said. 'I daresay we'll manage somehow. By the way, while I've got you on the phone, perhaps you could clear up a mystery that's been puzzling me. Are you, or are you not, having a thing with Neville Pratt?'

'Pratt?' she croaked. 'You must be joking. How could anyone have a thing with anyone with a name like that?'

I said, 'But you are having a thing with someone in Barfords?'

'No,' she said, 'I'm not.'

I said, 'Beddoes distinctly told me that somebody from the office came to your party the other night and played a leading role in your orgy.'

Sue said, 'Is everyone going round the twist? What orgy? We played Scrabble and danced a bit, that's all.'

'Never mind what you did or didn't do,' I said. 'Do you absolutely promise me that no one from the office came to your party?'

'Yes,' she said.

'And you're definitely not having a thing with anyone in the office?'

'No,' she said. And put the phone down on me.

Am seriously beginning to wonder if I might not be having a nervous breakdown without realizing it. They do say overwork can affect one in all sorts of strange ways.

Still, sufficiently *compos mentis*, I'm glad to say, to remember to ring Armitage re our proposed visit to a massage parlour. To judge from the enthusiasm with which he agreed to meet me on Tuesday afternoon, he must have been having a pretty lean time of it in the last few weeks, in every sense of the word. I reminded him that he had promised in return to give me Jane's telephone number, which he duly did.

'A bargain's a bargain,' he said.

'Not for some I know it isn't,' I said, and rang off.

Rang Jane on her 673 number, which I have a feeling is somewhere the other side of Clapham Common, but no reply. I can't quite remember now what it is I'm so keen to get in touch with her about.

Thought about ringing Beddoes in Brussels to challenge him over the Sue and Pratt business, but decided I had put up with enough flannel for one day and watched Melvyn Bragg's excellent arts programme instead.

What a clever young man he is. I bet he didn't get where he is today by wasting his time with second-rate has-beens. And neither in the future shall I.

Monday, 26 February

To Alma Mater for the day. Had every intention of setting off early. As Dickie Dunmow had said when I telephoned to confirm the arrangements, 'The sooner you get here, the sooner you can tell us what you want to know and the sooner we can decide whether we will tell you.'

Unfortunately, thanks to Sue's unexpected absence, was forced to spend two hours battling with Personnel over a temporary typist.

Miss Bintree finally agreed to release a dim but pretty creature called Una who, within five minutes of arriving in my office, had received visits from practically every messenger in the building, each one of whom actually had the sauce to claim to be her fiancé.

Finally became so incensed by sounds of giggling as I was trying to get through to Dickie re my slight change of plan that I was compelled to read the riot act. As luck would have it, the messenger in question turned out to be the spotty youth who had tried to make a monkey out of me over the matter of my mail.

I said in my iciest voice, 'I'm afraid my secretary has a great deal of work to do. If you must meet her, you're welcome to do so during the lunch hour. But, in the meantime, I must ask you to be about your business.'

I turned and walked back into my office. As I did so, the spotty messenger made a lavatorial noise. When I challenged him, he said, 'Oh didn't you know, Mr Mann? Una suffers from a rare stomach complaint. She's under the doctor. I don't think it's very nice of you to talk like that in front of her.'

The maddening thing is that he could have been telling the truth. However, I suspect from the smothered giggles that this youth is, for reasons that I cannot fathom, merely bent on confrontation at all costs. However, if he thinks he is going to get a rise out of me, he's got another think coming.

I said very quietly, 'If I catch you in here again for no good reason, you'll be suffering from a rare complaint of the backside.'

Meant of course that he would be feeling the end of my boot, but should have known that he would deliberately choose to misunderstand me.

'Fancy a bit of rough trade from time to time, do you squire?' he said, rolling his eyes suggestively.

I said, 'Any more lip out of you and I'll be speaking to the head of the post room about you.'

He said, 'Not before I've told him a thing or two about you and your nasty suggestions. And I've got a witness.'

Responded to this feeble attempt at blackmail with a brief look of withering scorn, and left for the fresh wholesome air of the Weald of Kent which I breathed so happily for four and a half happy years.

Parked in Pegram's Piece only to be informed by officious Under Magister that it was reserved for staff only. Luckily, he was not only unknown to me but several years younger and, when I pointed out that I was (a) an OF, (b) on school business *and* (c) had an appointment with Mr Dunmow, he quickly caved in. I thought he would.

Skirted Apthorpe's Bottom and bounded up front steps of School House like the young lion I once was. Entered Back Passage and was almost knocked down by gang of small boys running full tilt towards Toggers' Room. From sheer force of habit called out, 'No running in Back Passage!'

All the boys ran on heedlessly, except one, obviously a New Squit, who said, 'Who are you?'

I said, 'I'll show you who I am, you nasty little Squit,' and seizing him by the ear I marched him along to Toggers', threw open the door and pointed at the wall above the Old Fireplace where the house honours board hung, only to realize too late that I was pointing at a huge collage of nude pinups cut from girlie magazines.

I suppose in the circumstances I cannot blame the boy for crying out 'Help! Assault!' nor his chums for coming to his rescue. However, I still maintain it was not necessary for *all* twenty of them to use quite so much force to bring me to the floor, and I really do think they could have frogmarched me along to Dickie's study quite satisfactorily without going to the lengths of tying my thumbs behind my back.

It was a pity, too, that Dickie chose not to take a rather more severe line with them. The words, 'Hallo, Crisp. Started your researches already, I see,' could hardly fail to carry with them the implication of approval, however faint.

I might have expected him to assume that my sole purpose for being there was to dig up more dirt on the old homosexuality chestnut.

He said, 'I know you left-wing journalist types; always the first to pick on some trivial aspect of public school life and blow it up out of all proportion. Anything for a bit of sensationalism. Still, that's what sells papers, eh?'

Opened my mouth to put the record straight, but once Dickie gets a bee in his bonnet about something, it takes more than reasoned argument to shift it.

'The fact is,' he went on, 'the boys have got many better things to think about than sex.'

'Such as?' I said.

'The usual things,' he said, 'O and A levels, carpentry, the school play, rugger . . .'

I said that surely rugger was merely one of many substitutes for releasing sexual aggression.

Dickie said, 'I had hoped we might have been able to clear up this matter in a few minutes between ourselves, but you newshounds will never take anyone's word for anything will you? If you don't believe me, you might try talking to some of the boys. Beaumont and Fletcher have got free periods. They should be in their cubby now.'

He led the way up to Top Swine Level and knocked on the door of Big Cubby. From inside came the sound of scuffling and whispering, and finally one of them gave us permission to come in. They were both at their desks, apparently hard at work, but, to my way of thinking, looking rather flushed and guilty. Dickie said, 'This is Mr Crisp OF. He's doing an article about homosexuality in the public schools and he'd like to ask you a few questions.'

Could not help commenting on the eye-catching display of nude pinups with which every wall was covered.

Dickie said, 'A few comely females scantily clad can hardly be said to amount to wholesale depravity – especially as the display of . . . er . . . toilet areas is strictly forbidden.'

After he had gone, Beaumont said, 'The real stuff's behind you, if you're interested.'

I turned to find, sellotaped to the back of the door, half a dozen of the fullest frontal shots of women I have ever seen.

Fletcher said, 'Dickie never sees them because he always stands with the door open against the wall.'

Could not resist roaring with laughter and slapping my thighs, which obviously endeared me to the boys because they were soon revealing all sorts of fascinating things about what they really get up to in schools these days. For instance, most of the senior boys seem to have girlfriends in the girls' boarding school about three miles away.

Beaumont said, 'We can see them five times a week if we really feel like it.'

'Trouble is, we're usually too shagged,' said Fletcher.

'From rugger?' I said.

'No', said Beaumont. 'Wanking.'

They then told me that they have house and school dances once or even twice a term for Swine and upwards.

'Trouble is,' Fletcher said, 'they only give you a quarter of an hour after the dance for any unfinished business, so to speak.'

'The shed behind Upper Bummers is very popular,' said Beaumont.

'If you don't mind upper splinters in your upper bummer,' said Fletcher.

I said, 'According to Dickie, all this homosexual stuff is a thing of the past?'

'Oh, we still eye the New Squits and mark them out of ten,' said Fletcher.

'But it's nothing serious,' said Beaumont.

I said, 'You mean you don't get up to anything?'

'If we did,' said Beaumont, 'you don't think we'd tell you, do you?'

We all roared. Despite our age differences, I think we understood each other.

'Got a ciggy on you?' Beaumont said suddenly.

Was naturally hesitant about encouraging smoking in Cubbies but, as they pointed out, if only one smoked and someone came in, I could always say it was me.

As they were puffing away merrily, Fletcher said, 'How much will we get for all this?'

I said, 'Six of the best, I shouldn't wonder.'

Beaumont said, 'What Fletchy means was how much will your paper pay us for these sensational revelations?'

'Bearing in mind we might be among the ranks of the unemployed school leavers by this time next week,' added Fletcher.

I pointed out that I did not actually work for a paper and that there was no question of payment for information supplied for a survey of this kind.

Beaumont said, 'Mr Dunmow's going to be very upset

when we tell him how Mr Crisp OF offered us cigarettes in return for information, isn't he, Fletch?'

'Very,' said Fletcher.

Unfortunately, I could see their point.

The two of them whispered together for a while, then Fletcher said, 'Tell you what. Beau's been gated for the last week and he's rather anxious to see his girlfriend. Supposing we were to get a message to her, then you could drive across to Bedenham this afternoon during games, pick her up and bring her back here . If anyone challenges you, you can say she's your wife or your secretary. She'll stay for half an hour or so and then you can drive her back again.'

I said, 'I don't know if you are both planning to go into the blackmailing business when you leave here, but I suggest you try cutting your teeth on someone a good deal less gullible.' And with that I stood up and left the room.

Was crossing Apthorpe's Bottom just as the Refec Bell was ringing out from Tommy Tiddle, when I felt a pull on my sleeve and turned round to find it was the New Squit whose ear I had pinched earlier.

He pressed a pound note into my hand and said, 'Be a good chap and slip across to the newsagent's and get me the new *Men Only*, will you?'

Am not by nature a violent man, but there are occasions when even my patience is exhausted and a good sharp shock is more salutary than a thousand words of admonition.

As luck would have it, no sooner had the flat of my hand made contact with the back of the boy's head than round the corner appeared the very same boys who had come to his rescue in Toggers' earlier on. Decided discretion the better part of valour, and with cries of 'Help! Assault! Child-beater! Stop thief!' ringing in my ears, I legged it for Arthur's Opening.

Hurtled into Pegram's Piece only to find my car had disappeared. Not daring to stop, headed for Black Hole and ran straight into officious Under Magister who informed me coolly that, since I had chosen to break the rules about parking, he had asked the police to come and tow the vehicle away.

By now the boys had almost caught up with me. The Under Magister grabbed my coat; but I shook him off and ran like the devil towards Main Gate. Luckily, I managed to lose them all in the back streets of the town, but my luck was short-lived, since it cost me twenty quid to retrieve my car from the police pound.

How I can ever have spent the last twenty years singing the praises of the place I cannot imagine. Had I not already cancelled my subscription to the OF Society a year ago, I would have no hesitation in doing so here and now. I shall certainly make it quite clear that it is the last place for which I shall be entering my sons. If ever I have any, that is.

Halfway to London, it suddenly occurred to me, apropos of Beaumont and Fletcher's little ruse, that the only girls' school in the vicinity was at least twenty miles away, and it was not called Bedenham but High Heath. What their purpose can possibly have been in trying to persuade me otherwise is anybody's guess. Thank goodness my natural instinct to call their bluff did not let me down.

Tuesday

Arrived in the office this morning expecting to find the entire film section typed out and ready for Xeroxing, only to be told by Una that, because I hadn't told her whether I wanted it double or single spaced, she had decided to do nothing and wait until I got back.

I pointed out in terms that left her in little doubt as to my disappointment that the whole thing was due to be delivered tomorrow and that I had no alternative but to ask her to work through the lunch hour and, if necessary, right through the night. At which point she burst into floods of tears, said it was not her fault and that she had never worked for anyone so cruel in her life. And with that she gathered up her personal effects and left the room.

Realizing there was almost certainly no chance of getting anyone else in time, sat down there and then and started typing away as fast as is humanly possible with only two fingers. By lunchtime, had managed to produce eight reasonably clean pages. Rang Armitage to suggest postponing our massage parlour visit until another day.

He said, 'I haven't got another day.'

I said, in that case, would he mind if we didn't meet for lunch first.

'Not if you don't mind missing out on a certain amount of background material,' he said.

Had no alternative but to say I'd meet him in San Giuliano as agreed.

Typed out one more page, made a botch, tried to erase it, made a hole in the paper, threw it in the waste-paper basket and set off for Soho. Armitage already at the table nursing a Campari and soda and nibbling on *grissini*.

Had I the slightest inkling of what he was about to describe, I certainly would not have ordered a starter of the cured meat covered with olive oil and black pepper.

Had never realized before that he had travelled quite so extensively in the Far East, nor that he was in the habit of taking at least one holiday every year in Manila or Bangkok. In his estimation these are the sex capitals of the world.

'Never has a city been more aptly named,' he said.

'What?' I said. 'Manila?'

'No,' he said. 'Kuala Lumpur.' He then proceeded to describe in vivid detail a typical afternoon's visit to a typical oriental massage parlour.

Apparently the great trick is to pick out a couple of girls and get them to give you a Chinese Sandwich. This involves one of them lying down, the customer lying on top of her and then the second girl lying on top of the customer.

Could not quite make out what happens then, but gather everyone wriggles about a good deal and a jolly time is had by all.

I said, 'This is all very interesting, Armitage, but my report specifically covers the sexual life of the British.'

'Oh,' said Armitage blithely, 'I've never been to a place like that in London.'

'Why not?' I asked him.

'Well,' he said. 'It's always so cold isn't it?'

As I was paying the bill, remarked that I hoped that whatever he had laid on by way of a practical demonstration would represent considerably better value.

'I don't know what you mean,' he said. 'As a way of getting one into the right frame of mind, a good spicy Italian lunch with plenty of rough red wine takes a lot of beating.'

Did not like to say so, but have never felt less in a mood for anything in my life.

Was tempted on more than one occasion to dodge down a side alley, grab the first taxi that came my way and head back to the office and the IBM golf-ball. Yet something drew me on. Was it curiosity? Conscientiousness? An absurd wish not to let Armitage down? Even an unconscious message from my libido? Who knows? Perhaps a liberal helping of all four.

After a while I asked Armitage where he was taking me – Bangkok?

He said, 'I told you, I don't know the London scene. I thought we'd have a look around and pick one out at random.'

It was hardly the moment to remind him that the whole purpose of my asking him along was that one's path should be made smoother and easier through his knowledge and expertise, not rutted and potholed with doubt and uncertainty. If I had wanted the blind to lead the blind, I could have brought Mother.

Suddenly Armitage stopped dead in his tracks. 'This looks the sort of thing,' he said, peering in through a corner window hung with multicoloured strips of plastic.

'How do you know?' I asked him.

'They're all much of a muchness,' he said.

The sign above the main window proclaimed it to be the Scando-Thai Saunarama and Massage Centre.

It all sounded extremely respectable – so much so that I could not help but ask Armitage if he was sure this was quite the sort of place I had in mind.

Armitage said, 'Not losing your nerve by any chance, are you?'

I said that nothing could be further from my mind.

'Good,' he said. '*A nos moutons* then.' And before I knew what, we were through the door and standing in front of the reception desk where a sensible-looking girl in a white blouse and tweed skirt said, 'What did you two gentlemen have in mind?'

Armitage leered at her and said, 'What are you offering?'

She said, 'Royal Sauna, Massage and Shower is £15; VIP Assisted Sauna, Massage and Shower, with body shampoo and cologne, comes to £25.'

'What's the difference?' Armitage asked.

'The VIP's assisted, the Royal isn't,' she said.

Armitage said, 'Oh I think the assisted for us, don't you, Crisp?'

I said whatever was easiest.

'Makes no difference to us one way or the other,' said the receptionist.

I said that perhaps she could be a little more specific.

'Assisted includes hand relief,' she said. 'Extras have to be discussed and arranged with the girl in question.'

Felt like asking if I could forgo the hand relief in favour of an interview at the same price, but decided to play cards close to the chest at this stage of proceedings.

The girl said, 'So that'll be two assisted then?'

We both nodded.

'That'll be fifty pounds,' she said, 'including VAT.'

'And relief,' said Armitage.

I said that I was rather short of cash, as it happened, but she said I could pay by cheque with a cheque card or credit card, whichever I preferred. This is not the first time I have found myself reflecting what a strange world it is where one can get pleasure on credit.

She then showed us through to a small room with some rather cheap armchairs in one of which a dark-haired, plump young man was smoking a scented cigarette and watching a middle-aged woman on TV interviewing another woman with a large snake round her neck.

After a while, two girls came into the room. Both were dark-haired and both wore T-shirts and very short shorts. They introduced themselves as Carol and Liz. I thought I had rather the better of the bargain with Carol, but there wasn't a lot in it.

I remarked that I hoped we would be in separate rooms.

Liz said, 'What do you take us for?'

'We don't go in for kinks here,' Carol said.

I said, 'No chance of a Chinese Sandwich then?'

'Coffee, tea and soft drinks,' said Liz, 'but no food.'

Carol led me into a small room containing a wooden chair, a wash basin, a wooden trolley on wheels containing various powders and unguents, a small pile of towels and a box of Kleenex, and a couch of the sort you see in doctors' waiting rooms, covered with a white sheet. The decor consisted largely of nude girls swimming up a silver wall-paper.

Carol said, 'If you'd like to get undressed and lie on the table.'

'Completely?' I said.

She said, 'Well I can hardly be expected to give you a VIP Assisted in a double-breasted suit, now can I?'

Was standing there, feeling rather cold and foolish, when she suddenly said, 'Will you be requiring any extras?'

'Such as?' I said.

'That's up to you,' she said. 'French?'

'No, no,' I said. 'English and proud of it. Born just outside Chatham as a matter of fact. I can never remember whether that makes me a Kentish Man or a Man of Kent. Do you know that part of the world by any chance?'

She said that she was happy to say she had never been within fifty miles of Chatham and that she hadn't got all day and would I mind getting on the table, face down.

I said, as I settled myself on to the couch, 'I was wondering, do you see any moral dilemma in the job you do?'

'I see a lot of frustrated old sods,' she said, 'and a lot of overweight bodies. Not a lot else.'

I said, 'Wouldn't you say frustrated is a relative term?'

'All right then,' she said. 'Frustrated is a relative term. Talcum or Baby Oil?'

'What's the difference?' I said.

'Do you suffer from dry skin?' she said.

I said that I did rather.

'I'll give you the oil then,' she said, and took her T-shirt off.

Have often wondered how one would behave if one knew with absolute certainty that in the next few moments one was going to die. I imagine one's feelings are not dissimilar to those I experienced as Carol poured oil on to my back and started to rub up and down my spine. One simply closes one's eyes and says to oneself, 'This is it,' and awaits the inevitable. Was interested to note how calm I was. In fact, after a while, was beginning to feel extremely relaxed, not to say sleepy. I remember feeling a slightly different sensation in the small of my back and asked her what it was. I think she said something like 'Look, no

131

hands' and then I must have dozed off, because the next thing I knew she was manhandling me onto my back.

I heard her say, 'My, my, this won't do at all, Mr Crisp. We're going to have to try a little harder, aren't we?' when the most excruciating cramp shot through my leg.

Almost without thinking, leapt off the table and hobbled round the room, rubbing the back of my thigh and trying to straighten out my leg to relieve the pain. Unfortunately, in my agony, did not look where I was going and cannoned straight into Carol who fell backwards with a shriek onto the trolley which carried her headlong into the wall with a crash before hurling her senseless onto the floor.

I did not see there was any reason for the manager to take quite such a strong line with me. It was an accident, as I tried to explain, and I can't help thinking that Carol must experience many worse things in her line of business than a small bump on the head. I also think they might have permitted me to have a quick shower before getting dressed. Johnson's Baby Oil is all very well in its place, but not directly beneath a shirt and tie and double-breasted wool and worsted suit.

As for my demanding a proportion of my money back, I believe I was entirely justified. Apart from the lack of shower, I could hardly be said to be a satisfied customer in any sense of the word. May take the matter further or may not.

As I was being shown the door, Armitage appeared looking well pleased with himself. 'Judging from the noise,' he said, 'you got more than you bargained for.'

Couldn't be bothered to answer and, ignoring further enquiries, hobbled up the street in search of a taxi.

Was wrestling with the intricacies of golf-ball, page twelve of the report and continuing sharp pains in the thigh when Armitage rang to enquire after my health and to thank me for a most satisfactory afternoon.

I said, 'The only person whose health interests me round here is my secretary. She claims to have taken to her bed with flu.'

'Correction,' said Armitage. 'She has taken to *my* bed.'

'Since when?' I demanded.

'Since about a fortnight ago,' he said.

I said, 'You didn't happen to go to a party at her flat about ten days ago, did you?'

'Yes,' he said.

Have a feeling I may have damaged telephone in my anger.

Rang Beddoes from home on the cheap rate later that evening. I made it clear I was in no mood to beat about the bush.

'You told me that Pratt came round to Sue's party that night and misbehaved. Yet now I learn that it was, in fact, Armitage.'

Beddoes said, 'Oh I'm sorry if I misled you. I thought you asked me if he was a prat, and he was.'

Really, as if I could give a row of beans whether Sue is having a thing with Pratt, Armitage or the entire Australian cricket team. Here am I supposedly the leading expert on sex in Britain today, yet I have not had a thing with anyone for the last six weeks. Indeed, my sex drive has reached such an all-time low that I cannot even keep awake during a topless massage.

Steps will clearly have to be taken.

Wednesday

Today I am due to deliver the Crisp Report. Not only am I dead on my feet after an entire night at the golf-ball (and I'm still only on page 75), but I am suddenly convinced that a section on How to Improve Your Sex Life and Make Yourself More Attractive to the Opposite Sex is absolutely crucial to the report's success.

Home at six for a bath, shave and breakfast, then back at the keys by 7.30.

Called Miss Hippo at ten to assure her that report on its way. She said, 'Mr Hardacre is in Stockholm all this week. I'll give him your message when he comes in on Monday morning.'

I said, 'In that case, since I am without a secretary, I wonder if you would be kind enough to help me out with some typing?'

'I am a personal assistant,' Miss Hippo said, 'not a typist. There are plenty of those in the pool.' And she put the phone down on me.

Rang typing pool to be informed by Miss Bintree that, owing to illness, she was short-staffed as it was and that anyway she couldn't risk having any more of her girls upset.

Have worked out that, if I can keep up an average of forty-five pages a day for the next four days, that will give me just enough time to work up my remaining notes, and research and write Improvement Section. Where, though, to begin?

By an astonishing coincidence, was skimming through newspaper while tackling sardine and cucumber sandwich and coffee in O Sole Mio coffee bar, when what should my eye alight upon but an article about how a hairdresser called Ricci Burns transformed a young executive, not unlike myself, into a modern sex symbol. Cannot say that I have ever been a great fan of the boiler suit, nor is anyone likely to catch me mincing about with make-up all over my face. However, am most impressed by the tousled, devil-may-care hairstyle, and feel sure that to place oneself in Mr Burns' hands for an afternoon would prove a fascinating experiment.

Rang his PR who couldn't have been more helpful and made an appointment for me for four o'clock.

Arrived at his West End salon by taxi in pouring rain. Everything was white: walls, floor, furniture. Even the hairdressers were dressed in specially designed white creations.

Mr Burns, his white shirt contrasting magnificently with his lean, tanned face and his glossy black hair, rushed forward to greet me for all the world as if Mick Jagger had just walked in off the street.

It was all a far cry from Jack's round the corner from my flat, with his cracked basin, his Durex advertisements, his dog-eared pile of *Weekend* magazines, his nicotine-stained fingers and his perennial hacking cough.

First, I was handed over to a young man who made me sit with my head resting backwards over a basin while he gave my hair the most thorough washing of its life.

While waiting for Mr Burns to attend to me, I drank an excellent cup of coffee and tried to spot some of the famous film stars, TV personalities and beauties who have helped to make him the superstar among hairdressers that he is today. One blonde girl at the end reading *Vogue* might have been Liv Ullman, except that those sort of women tend to look the same with wet hair.

After about ten minutes, a young man came across and told me that Mr Burns was ready for me.

'Now, Mr Crisp,' he said. 'You're all mine.' And running his fingers through my locks, proceeded to insult Jack's handiwork in no uncertain terms. 'You've got a beautifully shaped head,' he told me, 'but no one's cut *into* your hair. They've just gone round the edges, as usual.'

Had not realized before that in this sort of place an assistant does all the donkey-work of actually holding your hair, while the great man himself merely wields the scissors.

I cannot pretend that, after years of Jack's heavy-handed assaults on my hair, I responded naturally to such luxury, but the experience was not an unpleasant one, and I must admit that the carefree styling did give me a certain youthful *je ne sais quoi*.

I did enquire about make-up, simply out of curiosity, but Ricci said that, apart from face-bronzing gel and eyelash dye, make-up for men was not nearly as popular as one might think.

I said that I was very glad to hear it, but supposing someone were to come to him and ask him to give them a few simple hints on how to make himself more attractive to women, what would he suggest?

He thought for a moment and said. 'A good haircut, a fortnight's diet, regular exercise, and self-confidence – though that probably comes with the other three.'

I said, 'All right. We've dealt with the hair; what about the rest?'

Ricci looked me up and down and said, 'If I were you, I'd start off with a simple diet – an orange and black coffee for breakfast, cottage cheese and an apple for lunch, and chicken, fish or meat and plenty of green vegetables for dinner. Then I'd take myself off to a good health club, like that one in Kensington, where they have a gym, sauna, massage, sunbeds and so on. Then I'd buy myself some nice clothes, a nice pair of jeans, a polo neck sweater, a nice belt, you know. I'd have lunch with Molly Parkin. Oh, and I'd start taking ginseng. It does wonders for your libido.'

I pointed out that I wasn't really asking for myself. It was all hypothetical and in the interests of research.

'You could have fooled me,' he said.

Am not used to being spoken to this way by hair-dressers. However, at that moment he informed me that the whole thing was on the house. I have never been one to look a gift horse in the mouth and, at £20 a haircut and with the whole expenses issue balanced on a knife edge, this was not the moment to start doing so.

Normally, would have had no hesitation in taking a taxi home, but this evening, anxious to check women's reaction to my new looks, plumped instead for tube. Interested to notice that not a single woman gave me so much as a second glace. Of course it *was* the height of the rush hour. The only positive reaction came from a burly working type who I bumped into by mistake on the escalator in my anxiety to get to the chemist before the shops shut.

'Sorry,' I called after me.

'Get out of it, you poof,' he called back.

Thank heavens I'd had the foresight not to try the make-up.

Bought box of ginseng tablets, half a dozen large oranges and a pound of sprouts to go with the rump steak in my deep-freeze compartment. Also made slight detour and called in at health club.

It is obviously extremely well-equipped, and the people who run it appear to know what they are talking about. The atmosphere is casual and friendly and, if the signed photographs of film and TV celebrities that line the stairs to the gym are any indication of the type of clientele one can expect to rub shoulders with in the sauna bath, this could well turn out to be very much my sort of place. £190 a year seems little enough to shell out for a healthy body. It's not quite White's, but the people who sit about in leather armchairs in St James's do not do so in order to improve their sex lives.

At all events, took a brochure and said I'll ring tomorrow and talk further.

Arrived home starving and opened freezer compartment to find steak gone and note saying, 'Man cannot live by bread alone, laddie, especially with a lady to entertain. Cheers, Ralph.'

Am glad now I decided to keep the hundred pounds.

Potatoes obviously out of the question, so had to content myself with huge plate of sprouts. Dull but nutritious.

After *Nine O'Clock News*, took my first ginseng tablet. Have never had a lot of time for orientals. However, when it comes to sex, am perfectly prepared to bow to their superior wisdom. Ginseng is not called 'The Man Root' for nothing. Indeed, I had erotic thoughts for the rest of the evening, especially about Jane. She seems to be constantly in the forefront of my mind these days.

Rang her number on off-chance but no reply.

Also mystified by Ricci Burns' suggestion re lunch with Molly Parkin. Is one to understand that this might lead to useful information for the report or what?

To bed in puzzled mood – also with slightly gippy tummy. Am wondering if ginseng is not just another form of natural laxative. If so, what possible reason could Ricci have had for recommending it? There's nothing sexy about senna pods.

Thursday

Arrived at office at 7.30 and straight to golf-ball. By 10.15 had completed ten more pages and had obtained Molly's phone number from Ricci's PR.

For some reason got it into her head that I was an obscene book salesman. Fortunately, we were able to uncross our lines before too much damage was done, and she has agreed to meet me for lunch at Langan's Brasserie. One is always reading about this place in the newspapers. I understand it to be a haunt of the rich, famous and trendy, but have never had the opportunity to try it out for myself.

She said, 'Langan's is very sexy. You've got to be sure and make a good entrance, though. In a big hat preferably.'

Frankly, it's all gobbledygook to me, but affected to be familiar with modern café society language and, when she asked exactly what it was I wanted to know, I said cryptically, 'Everything.'

I think she's intrigued and puzzled. I can't say I'm surprised. I'm pretty much out of my depth myself. In fact, the longer I continue with the subject, the more I have the feeling that everything is getting slightly out of hand.

But then isn't sex most of the time?

Typed furiously till one when bought a Cox's Orange Pippin and a small pot of cottage cheese from nearby delicatessen. Tummy still rather wobbly but at the same time feeling altogether more lithe and on my toes. Normally never give any of the secretaries a second glance in the lift, yet this morning caught myself treating Caroline from Personnel to one of the frankest and most searching looks I have ever given anyone. Pleased to note from the puzzled expression on her face that my essential masculinity had struck home in no uncertain terms.

After a while, she said, 'What have you done to your hair?'

I said, 'Nothing much. I just thought it was time I gave it a little pzazz. Do you like it?'

'I'm not sure,' she said.

She was obviously so intrigued she completely missed her floor. I shouldn't be at all surprised if this little encounter doesn't bear fruit before very long.

As the senior instructor at the health club reminded me when I called round in the afternoon for a chat, 'A really fit man is like a thoroughbred stallion in looks and performance. Stamina on the exercise machines means stamina in bed, believe you me.'

Am not sure I'm prepared to put in a three-hour routine three times a week for five years like the muscle-bound hulk with the spotty back I watched lifting seventy kilos on the lateral pull-down machine. But then, as the instructor said, 'These tasty young birds don't want a gorilla on their hands.'

Have told them I will make a definite decision re membership first thing Monday morning. The odd thing is that I was only in the place for a few minutes yet I feel fitter already.

Am up to page 145. Only another hundred to go.

Friday

Lunch with Molly Parkin informative, encouraging and unnerving, all at the same time.

Surprised to discover my blue motorcycling outfit caused even more heads to turn than her gold sou'wester. I had the devil's own job trying to persuade her that, while eminently practical at 30 mph in driving rain, it did not make for ideal luncheon wear.

At all events, we had a fascinating chat. She was particularly sound on how to attract members of the opposite sex. She said that the more sexually active one is, the stronger the sexual scent one puts out and the more likely one is to 'pull something' as she so quaintly puts it.

Meanwhile, she has suggested a routine that she assures me is an absolute winner every time:

1. The moment you meet a girl, look her straight in the eye.
2. Let your eyes drop to her lips.
3. Go back to her eyes. All this should take a matter of seconds.
4. Drop your gaze discreetly to her bosom. By this stage she should have a reasonable inkling of what you have in mind.
5. Weigh in with a complimentary remark, such as, 'What a great haircut; where did you have it done?' She now knows you are more aware of her body than her mind.
6. Get cracking with the chat. There is no greater aphrodisiac than talking about oneself, so get her to do just that.

For some people, apparently, all this comes as second nature, but those of more reticent disposition should practise first in front of a mirror.

Could not take my eyes off her lips and bosom for the rest of the meal, but obviously it was a bit late for all that and, when I went to peck her on the cheek as we were leaving, she shook me firmly by the hand and marched off to look for a taxi. I took it as a compliment to my professionalism.

Stayed on in the office till nearly eight and managed to get to page 170. Took golf-ball, plus notes, paper, correcting fluid etc. home with me in a taxi.

Thank heavens for the ginseng. It's certainly given me the extra energy I need. Sat through TV this evening till after eleven without falling asleep once. Tummy still slightly on the move. Am wondering if sprouts three nights running is really wise. May very well switch to cauliflower tomorrow. Or possibly even carrots.

Practised eye movements briefly in front of bathroom mirror but my heart not really in it.

To bed with a glass of unsweetened lemon juice and the *TV Times*. I don't know which sets my teeth on edge more.

Saturday

Woke feeling as if someone had hit me over the head with a sandbag, only to discover to my horror that it was 2.15 in the afternoon.

Had no sooner got down to typing at three than power failure put paid to chances of catching up on nearly four hours' worth of lost time.

Was groping way to kitchen in dark when phone rang. It was Jane to say that she was just back from an extended skiing holiday and had heard from the Pedalows that I was anxious to get hold of her.

I do not believe I have ever been more relieved to hear anyone's voice than I was to hear hers at that moment. Have always believed that, deep down inside, she and I were really meant for each other all along. For two pins would have chucked golf-ball, typed pages, notes and everything else to do with this assignment clean out of the window and rushed round to her there and then, had she not already arranged to have dinner with her brother.

Remembering his talent for bumming lifts off people etc, I said, 'Just as long as he's not planning on taking you somewhere cheap and cheerful round here. We're having a power cut.'

She said, 'Actually we're going to the Connaught.'

'The Connaught?' I exclaimed. 'Your brother?'

'What's so extraordinary about that?' she said. 'His car hire business is doing very well.'

I said I was glad to know I wasn't the only one whose career had blossomed.

We have arranged to meet on Monday evening for a drink at the Piccadilly Hotel. Am so excited I can hardly think of anything else.

Even so, the moment lights came on again, applied my

mind once more to task in hand, and by two a.m. had reached page 200.

Would have had quick mirror practice before turning in, but by then eyes capable of only one movement.

Sunday

Had most erotic dream about Jane I have ever known. Am not sure what I have to thank for it. Who cares? All I do know is that, the moment when I erased the last typing error and banged down the last full stop of the Crisp Report was, for me, one of the high spots of my marketing career.

One hears it said that writing a book is rather like having a baby. I have always thought that, as similes go, this one oversteps the mark. All I can say is that, having suffered the birth pangs myself and known the joy of seeing the fruits of my labour lying in a neat pile beside the typewriter, I shall definitely take care not to get pregnant again for a very long time!

Monday, 5 March

Woke at six. Quite unable to get back to sleep again for excitement.

Up finally twenty minutes later for a long eye-movement session. One of them seems to be rather sore. Hope I haven't been overdoing it.

Am now into fifth day of diet and ginseng and, eye apart, have never felt fitter or more cheerful in my life.

Arrived at work bang on dot of nine, dropped off golf-ball and marched straight up to Hardacre's office. No sign of anyone, so dumped report firmly on middle of his desk where he can't possibly miss it.

By way of celebration, had white coffee with sugar from machine.

The moment I got into my room, wrote off to health club enclosing entrance form and cheque for £190.

Thought I might slip down there for a spot of weight training during lunch hour.

Was in fact on way out to buy track suit, gym shoes

etc. shortly after noon when Miss Hippo rang to say she had Keith Hardacre for me.

Could not conceal my glee as I said, 'Morning Keith. Any comments?'

He said, 'Not really, except to thank you for all the hard work you've put in and to tell you that, unfortunately, we have decided we won't be going ahead with the report after all.'

I said, 'I'm sorry Keith, I'm not with you. What do you mean we won't be going ahead? We *have* gone ahead. At least, *I* have. What do you think all those bits of paper on your desk are?'

Keith said, 'Yes, well, they certainly look interesting from what I've managed to skim so far. Some of it will come in useful as a starting point if ever we decide to go ahead at a later date.'

'What do you mean, starting point?' I said. 'I've been knocking myself out for six weeks over this.'

'And don't think we don't appreciate it,' said Keith. 'Of course, I realize now we should never have expected you to do any more than scratch the surface. It's obviously far too big a subject for one person to cover fully. Silly to have thought otherwise really. Still, it's all good experience after all, and I daresay there were a few fringe benefits to be enjoyed along the way. Now then, I'd like you to liaise with Pratt. I think you'll find he's got some interesting ideas for a new marketing strategy for Scandinavia. You'll be working with him again, so if you wouldn't mind moving back to your old office as soon as possible. By the way, an old colleague of yours from Harley Preston is joining us today on the sales side. Colin Armitage. First-class fellow.'

I may resign or I may not. It depends on the sort of response I get from the various publishers when I present them with the manuscript of my journal. Barfords may not recognize a best seller when they see one, but I can think of one or two people who will.

Anyway, was far too excited at the prospect of meeting Jane again to give a hoot one way or the other.

In the event, barely recognized her. I thought she had improved out of recognition when I saw her last year at the Pedalows', but that was without the deep Alpine suntan.

Was so taken aback I almost forgot the eye routine.

'What a great suntan,' I said, when I had completed it. 'Where did you get it?'

'I've already told you,' she said. 'I've been skiing. And why are you leering at me in that horrible way, Simon? It makes you look like those middle-aged men you see outside dirty cinemas. And what *have* you done to your hair?'

I said, 'I suppose you're going to tell me you don't like that either?'

'Not at all,' she said. 'It's wonderful. It makes you look ten years younger. You've lost some weight too. It suits you. Very sexy. I could quite fancy you.'

I often think life is like a huge elephant. One minute it is trampling you underfoot, scarcely aware of your existence; the next it has seized you by its trunk and lifted you gently and triumphantly onto its broad, safe, comfortable back.

Was naturally disappointed when Jane told me about the Austrian ski instructor and the baby she is expecting in a few months' time. Personally, I can think of many places I'd rather set up home in than Obergurgl.

On the other hand, find I am able to absorb the shock of her news with an insouciance of which I would have been quite incapable only a few weeks ago. The instructor at the health club was right. You're only as good as you feel, and I do not believe I have ever felt leaner, fitter and more virile in my life. Think big and think positive; that's my motto from now on.

I may decide to pop out to Obergurgl and sort the matter out with Hans, man to man, or I may not.

Jane is not the only fish in the sea by a long chalk and, with a potential best seller on my hands, I shall soon be in a position to pick and choose women at will.

Barfords' loss is certainly going to be my gain in every sense of the word.

First things first, though; I must sort out these wretched expenses.